Bluegrass Music Festivals
1996 Guide for U.S. & Canada

compiled & edited by
Michael & Joanne Stepaniak

Shoreline Publishing Company
Oak Park, Illinois

Shoreline Publishing Company
400 Forest Avenue
Oak Park, Illinois 60302 USA

ISBN 1-57067-016-1
ISSN 1084-7375

The front cover photo was taken at the Annual Museum of Appalachia's 1994 Tennessee Fall Homecoming in Norris, Tennessee. Bill Monroe, "the father of bluegrass music," performs during the all-day rain on Sunday. See page 76 for information on this event which features over 250 old-time musicians and hundreds of mountain craftspeople. Photo by Museum Founder/Director, John Rice Irwin.

The back cover photo is of Mac Martin and The Dixie Travelers after completing a bluegrass workshop at the Calliope Smoky City Folk Festival in Pittsburgh, Pennsylvania. Photo by Michael Stepaniak.

Cover design: Carol Simpson Productions

Interior design and typesetting: Stepaniak Enterprises

Receive **FREE PUBLICITY** for your event(s) and help us to expand the *Bluegrass Music Festivals Guide for U.S. & Canada*. Please write to us to request an information survey form(s) for the **1997** edition of the guide. Requests for survey forms must be received by **July 15, 1997**. There is no fee for these listings, but your survey form MUST be returned to us on or before **August 20, 1997** for inclusion in the 1997 edition.

To request a survey form for your festival(s), write to:

Michael Stepaniak
Bluegrass Music Festivals Guide
P.O. Box 82663
Swissvale, PA 15218

PREFACE

Bluegrass music is a unique, American innovation. Its roots, however, are an eclectic mix stemming from the musical traditions of the English, Irish and Scottish immigrants who settled in the Southern Appalachian Mountains. Combined with distinct influences from gospel music and Southern blues, the fundamental elements of what is now known worldwide as bluegrass music emerged in the late 1930s with the work of the Monroe brothers, Bill and Charlie. In 1938 the Monroe brothers separated and took their own paths. Bill Monroe, the acknowledged "Father of Bluegrass," formed The Blue Grass Boys, and in 1939 the group began playing regularly on WSM's Grand Ole Opry in Nashville, Tennessee.

In 1941 The Blue Grass Boys started touring extensively throughout the South, utilizing a large circus tent which was set up and torn down in each small town where they played. This was reminiscent of the traveling minstrel and revival shows that were common in the region. Nevertheless, it was not until 1945 that the characteristic sound of traditional bluegrass music was crystallized by Bill Monroe and The Blue Grass Boys during their performances on the Grand Ole Opry. Between 1945 and 1948, the teaming up of Lester Flatt on guitar, Bill Monroe on mandolin, Earl Scruggs on banjo, Howard "Cedric Rainwater" Watts on bass, and Chubby Wise on fiddle, further refined and solidified the sound that future generations would come to identify with bluegrass music.

A key feature of the bluegrass vocal style is the integration of multiple harmonies incorporating the phrasing and timing of old Southern blues and gospel music, sung in a high pitch reminiscent of Scottish bagpipes. A notable trait of traditional bluegrass music is the primary use of nonelectric stringed instruments. Bluegrass bands are commonly comprised of a guitar, fiddle, mandolin, upright bass, and the five-string banjo played in a three-finger picking style perfected and popularized by Earl Scruggs. Contrary to other forms of mountain music, bluegrass has embraced the banjo as a major solo or lead instrument. Other instruments may also be employed including the dobro, introduced to bluegrass music in 1955 by The Foggy Mountain Boys (the band formed by Flatt and Scruggs), mouth harp, jew's harp, autoharp, accordion, drums and piano.

At various times, each instrument in a bluegrass ensemble can act as a lead, backup, or rhythmic accompaniment. Therefore, bluegrass appeals to musical virtuosos who are attracted to its disciplined and competitive playing style. Because of its intricate demands on precision, bluegrass has been equated with chamber music. It has also drawn comparisons to jazz because of its hot licks, dynamic improvisational elements, and solos known as *breakdowns*.

According to Robert Cantwell, author of *Bluegrass Breakdown, The Making of The Old Southern Sound*, Bill Monroe created bluegrass as a method to "play old-time music in the modern world." In an interview with a reporter from *The Baltimore Sun* in 1977, Bill Monroe defined bluegrass as "the old Southern sound that was heard years ago, many, many years ago in the backwoods at country dances... Bluegrass brings out the old tones, ancient tones."

Today's bluegrass festivals are a natural outgrowth of their humble Southern origins, combining the best of minstrel shows, revival meetings and church socials. Bluegrass music is played and listened to by people of all ages and backgrounds, with its popularity growing extensively in both rural and urban settings. Bluegrass music is a true American original steeped in tradition which has become a vital and significant part of the world's colorful musical heritage.

Bluegrass music festivals are provided for the enjoyment of their audiences and their participants, and are a means to preserve, promote and perpetuate bluegrass music, one of our invaluable cultural treasures. We hope this guide makes your travels more enjoyable and your life richer for having experienced the joys of bluegrass music.

Michael & Joanne Stepaniak, editors

We wrote to festivals requesting that our survey form be completed and returned. Sometimes, however, the survey was not returned to us or was not fully completed. Consequently, some festivals are not listed or there are some gaps in the information provided. We apologize for any omissions, and invite you to let us know about festivals you would like to see included in next year's guide. Each festival must complete a survey form for inclusion. In order for us to contact a festival you would like to see listed in our guide, please send us the name of the festival, a contact name (if available), and a complete mailing address. We welcome your help in keeping this guide as complete and current as possible. You can write to us at:

Michael Stepaniak
Bluegrass Music Festivals Guide
P.O. Box 82663
Swissvale, PA 15218

CONTENTS

U.S. FESTIVALS 9-92

CANADIAN FESTIVALS 92-95

Festivals by Month 96–110

Late Arrivals 110

Order Form 111

A = wheelchair accessible   I = interpreter for hearing impaired   F = food   FF = fast food   EF = ethnic food
VF = vegetarian food   RF = regional food   R = restaurants nearby   P = pets welcome   CC = credit cards

Alabama

SEMI-ANNUAL BLUEGRASS SUPERJAM
April 5-6, November 1-2
Cullman County Agricultural Trade Center, Hwy. 31 North, Cullman, AL

Since 1982. Annual attendance is 5,000. This is Alabama's largest and most successful indoor festival. The Superjam was recently awarded a Top Twenty Event in the South by the Southeastern Tourism Society. Features bluegrass and gospel music. Past performers: Bill Monroe, Jim & Jesse, Mac Wiseman, Ralph Stanley, Nashville Bluegrass Band, and many other regional and local talent. All performances held indoors. Crafts area. Hours: Friday 6 p.m.-11 p.m., Saturday noon-11 p.m. Call for ticket prices. Advance ticket sales available. A, FF, R, MR, CO, CN, RVO, RVN, HN, M

Contact: Col. Chuck Carpenter, Bull City Productions, P.O. Box 1464, Cullman, AL 35056 • Phone: 205-747-1650 or 205-734-1556 or 205-734-0454

BLUFF CREEK BLUEGRASS FESTIVAL
May 31-June 1; September 27-28
Bluff Creek Music Park, Phil Campbell, AL

Since 1994. Annual attendance is 2,000. Features traditional and hard driving bluegrass music in a natural, scenic environment. This year's headliners: Jacob Landers, Southern Stranger. Past performers: Osborne Brothers, Bluegrass Cardinals. Crafts area. Performances held both indoors and outdoors. Hours: Friday 7 p.m. to ??; Saturday 1 p.m. to 6 p.m., and 7 p.m. to ??. Prices: Friday $8, Saturday $12. Advance ticket sales available. A, F (full meals), P (on leash), MR, CO, S, RVO, HO, M

Contact: Lonnie & Helen Strickland, Bluff Creek Music Park, Rt. 2, Box 184, Phil Campbell, AL 35581 • Phone: 205-993-4471

FOGGY HOLLOW BLUEGRASS GATHERIN'
June 7-8, September 27-28
Foggy Hollow Farm, btwn. Gadsden & Anniston, Webster's Chapel, AL

Since 1992. Annual attendance is 4,000. This great family-style bluegrass festival features plenty of campsite pickin', a full children's stage (with juggler, magician, clown and storyteller), and an all-around fabulous atmosphere. This year's headliners include Osborne Brothers, Claire Lynch, IIIrd Tyme Out, Tony Rice, Glen Tolbert, Distant Cousins, and Foggy Hollow Allstars. Past performers: Alison Krauss, Tony Rice, Cox Family, IIIrd Tyme Out, Country Gentlemen, Del McCoury Band, Carolina, Warrior River Boys, Sand Mountain Boys. Workshops, crafts and traditional dancing. All performances held outdoors. Festival runs from Friday 6 p.m. through Saturday midnight. Tickets: Friday $7 in advance, $10 at the gate; Saturday $12 in advance, $15 at the gate. Two-day pass $15 in advance, $18 at the gate. A, FF, R, P (not in stage area), MR, RR, CO, CN, S, RVO, RVN, HO, HN, M

MR = modern restrooms   RR = rustic restrooms   CO = camping on-site   CN = camping nearby   S = hot showers
RVO = RVs on-site   RVN = RVs nearby   HO = hookups on-site   HN = hookups nearby   M = motels nearby

Contact: Glen Williams or David Boley, Foggy Hollow Bluegrass Gatherin', 439 Ross Lake Road, Wellington, AL 36279 • Phone: 205-492-3700 or 205-442-1349

OLD YORK USA ANNUAL BLUEGRASS FESTIVAL
April 26-27
10 miles south of Jasper, Hwy. 69 S., Oakman, AL

Since 1995. Annual attendance 2,500. Old York USA is a recreated Wild West town, complete with boardwalk, saloon girls, cowboys, and a shoot-out at high noon. Located on the site of one of the oldest settlements in the state of Alabama. Only in its second year, this festival has received many favorable comments from past attendees! This year's headliners: Scott Vestal, David Parmley & Continental Divide, Larry Stephenson Band, Southern Blend, Lickety Split, Jake Landers Band, Herschel Sizemore Band, Sand Mountain Boys, Bluegrass Edition. Past performers: Del McCoury, Larry Stephenson, New Coon Creek Girls, Glen Duncan, Larry Cordle, and Lonesome Standard Time. Children's activities. Informal dancing. All performances held outdoors. Hours: Friday 7-11 p.m., Saturday 10 a.m.-11 p.m. Tickets: Friday $10, Saturday $14, weekend pass $20. Advance ticket sales available. A, FF, RF, R, CC, MR, RR, CO, S, RVO, HO, M

Contact: Bull Corry, P.O. Box 244, Oakman, AL 35579 • Phone: 205-622-3951

SOUTH ALABAMA BLUEGRASS CONVENTION AND FIDDLER'S CHAMPIONSHIP
July 20
Escambia County High School, Atmore, AL

Since 1979. Annual attendance is 900. Features the best in Southern Bluegrass performed by non-professionals as they compete for first place in the following competitions: string band, vocal band, harmonica, mandolin, banjo, guitar, and fiddle. Over $1,700 in cash is awarded to winners. All performances are held indoors. Hours are 5 p.m.-11 p.m. Tickets are $5 for adults, and $2.50 for children (12 and under). Advance ticket sales available. A, RF, R, MR, RVN, HN, M

Contact: Jerry Gehman, 201 12th Avenue, Atmore, AL 36502 • Phone: 334-368-8438 • Fax: 334-368-4454

TENNESSEE VALLEY OLD TIME FIDDLERS CONVENTION
October 4-5
Athens State College, Athens, AL

Since 1966. Annual attendance is 10,000 to 12,000. This festival is known as the "Grandaddy of Mid-South Fiddlers Conventions," and has been instrumental in reviving and preserving the tradition of competition in old time music. Over 200 contestants vie for cash prizes in a wide range of old time musical events. Craftsmen from around the area display their arts and crafts at the annual arts and crafts fair held in conjunction with the musical competition. Contest begins Friday 7 p.m. and

---

A = wheelchair accessible   I = interpreter for hearing impaired   F = food   FF = fast food   EF = ethnic food
VF = vegetarian food   RF = regional food   R = restaurants nearby   P = pets welcome   CC = credit cards

Saturday at 9:00 a.m. Admission: $3 Friday, $4 Saturday, or combination ticket for both days $6. A, F, R, MR, RR, CO (self-contained campers), RVN, M

Contact: Ewell P. Smith, 300 N. Beaty Street, Athens, AL 35611 • Phone: 205-233-8205 • Fax: 205-233-8164

Arizona

4 CORNER STATES BLUEGRASS FESTIVAL
November 8-10
Constellation Park, Wickenburg, AZ

Since 1979. Annual attendance is 4,500. This is the oldest bluegrass festival in Arizona and is held in the historic, 132 year-old community of Wickenburg. Thirteen contests for musicians to compete for over $6,500 in prize money. Past performers include the Bluegrass Patriots, Julie Wingfield, Loose Ties, Flint Hill, Pick It Here, Morton Brothers, Upstairs String Band, Weary Hearts, Scenic Route, Copperline, Jethro Burns, and U.S. Air Force Band Wild Blue Country. Festival hours are Friday noon-5 p.m., Saturday 8 a.m.-6 p.m., 7:30 p.m.-10 p.m., Sunday 8 a.m.-5 p.m. Friday ticket prices: adults $6, seniors (60+) $5, children (under 12) $3. Saturday and Sunday ticket prices: adults $8, seniors (60+) $7, children (under 12) $5. Saturday evening concert only is $5. Two-day, three-day and family discount passes. Advance ticket sales available. Musical competitions, children's activities and crafts area. All performances are held outdoors, except for the Saturday evening concert. A, FF, R, P (on leash), CC, MR, RR, CO (advance reservations), RVO, RVN, HN, M

Contact: Julie Brooks, P.O. Drawer CC, Wickenburg, AZ 85358 • Phone: 520-684-5479 • Fax: 520-684-5470

Arkansas

LAKEVIEW BLUEGRASS MUSIC FESTIVAL
September 26-28
Lakeview Park, Waldron, AR

Since 1987. Annual attendance is 1,000. A good family atmosphere and great bluegrass music along a lake. Past performers: Chubby Wise, Bluegrass Thoroughbreds, Don Wiley, Bill Grant & Delia Bell, Louisiana Grass. Crafts area. All performances held outdoors. Hours: 26th 6:30 p.m.-midnight, 27th 1 p.m.-midnight, 28th 1 p.m.-midnight. Tickets: Thursday $5, Friday $7, Saturday $8. A, FF, R, P (on leash), MR, S, RVO, RVN, HO, HN, M

Contact: Shirley Oliver, Lakeview Bluegrass Music Festival, Rt. 3, Box 44-S, Waldron, AR 72958 • Phone: 501-923-4217

MR = modern restrooms   RR = rustic restrooms   CO = camping on-site   CN = camping nearby   S = hot showers
RVO = RVs on-site   RVN = RVs nearby   HO = hookups on-site   HN = hookups nearby   M = motels nearby

ORIGINAL OZARK FOLK FESTIVAL
September 26–29
City Auditorium, Eureka Springs, AR

Since 1946. This is the oldest continuous folk festival in the Midwest. Features bluegrass, folk and other acoustic music. Past performers: Bill Monroe, Jim & Jesse, John Hartford, Leo Kottke, Tim & Mollie O'Brien, Nashville Bluegrass Band, Norman Blake, Maura O'Connell (1995 headliner). Musical competitions, workshops and dancing (clogging). Performances held both indoors and outdoors. Hours vary. Tickets: $8 to $15 per show, depending upon performances. Advance ticket sales available. A, R (all around town), CC, MR, CN, RVN, HN, M

Contact: Sandi Slaton, Original Ozark Folk Festival, P.O. Box 88, Eureka Springs, AR 72632 • Phone: 501-253-8737

California

18TH ANNUAL HUMBOLDT FOLKLIFE FESTIVAL
August 24
Adorni Center, Eureka, CA

Since 1979. Annual attendance is 2,000 to 5,000. This is a community event situated in a beautiful park on the Humboldt Bay. The sun shines, boats sail by, pelicans fish. One can hear any kind of traditional, non-traditional, old-time, bluegrass, modern bluegrass, ethnic or folk music, participate in terrific workshops, or dance the whole day long! Workshops, children's activities, crafts and dancing (traditional, ethnic, swing). Performances are both indoors and outdoors, with a covered area for the audience outdoors. Hours: 10 a.m.–11 p.m. Admission is free. A, FF, EF, VF, RF, R, MR, CN, RVN, HN, M

Contact: Paul Sheldon, Annual Humboldt Folklife Festival, P.O. Box 1061, Arcata, CA 95518 • Phone: 707-822-5394 • Fax: same (call first)

21ST ANNUAL CBA FATHER'S DAY BLUEGRASS FESTIVAL
June 13–16
Nevada County Fairgrounds, Grass Valley, CA

Since 1976. Annual attendance is 5,000 to 7,000. This is the oldest bluegrass festival in California. It is sponsored by the California Bluegrass Association, a nonprofit, all volunteer organization which presents a family-oriented festival. Four full days of music on stage and a four-day children's program. No alcohol is sold on the grounds. Ice chests are allowed. Features bluegrass and old-time Appalachian music. This year's headliners: Doyle Lawson & Quicksilver, The Osborne Brothers, Mac Wiseman, IIIrd Tyme Out. Past performers: Nashville Bluegrass Band, Bass Mountain Boys, Traditional Grass, Jim & Jesse, The Del McCoury Band. All performances held

---

A = wheelchair accessible   I = interpreter for hearing impaired   F = food   FF = fast food   EF = ethnic food
VF = vegetarian food   RF = regional food   R = restaurants nearby   P = pets welcome   CC = credit cards

outdoors. Workshops and crafts area. Between 12 and 13 food vendors. Hours: Thursday through Saturday 10 a.m.-11 p.m., Sunday 9:30 a.m.-7:30 p.m. Tickets: 4-day at the gate $70, 3-day at the gate $60. Discounts on early bird (thru 2/28) and advance. Also member discounts. A, FF, EF, VF, R, MR, RR, CO, CN, S (sometimes), RVO, RVN, HO (limited), HN (KOA 25 miles), M

Contact: Suzanne Denison, P.O. Box 304, Wilseyville, CA 95257 • Phone: 209-293-1559 • Fax: 209-293-1220

36TH TOPANGA BANJO & FIDDLE CONTEST DANCE & FOLK ARTS FESTIVAL
May 19
Paramount Ranch, Santa Monica Mountains, Agoura, CA

Since 1961. Annual attendance is 4,000. Features bluegrass, traditional, old time string band, and folk music. All levels of competition (beginning, intermediate and advanced). Offers a great variety of activities: 115 contestants on main stage, workshops, dance stage (demonstrations and participation), crafts booths, and jamming. Past performers: Phil Salazar Band, Tom Ball & Kenny Salton, Grateful Dudes, Crossroads. Children's activities and dancing (folk, traditional and ethnic). All performances and activities are held outdoors. Hours: 9 a.m.-6 p.m. Tickets: $7 (18-65), $2 (12-17 and 65+), free (under 12). A, FF, VF, R, P (on leash), MR, RR, M

Contact: Dorian & Dalia Keyser, Topanga Banjo & Fiddle Contest, P.O. Box 571955, Tarzana, CA 91356 • Phone: 818-382-4819 (hotline) or 818-345-3795

"COLORADO RIVER COUNTRY" MUSIC FESTIVAL
January 19-21
Colorado River Fair Grounds, Blythe, CA

Since 1988. Annual attendance is approx. 5,000. The festival furnishes wood and burners for jamming fires. The camping area is close to the festival stage. Two stages are going at all times. Nine categories of competition. Everyone is made to feel welcome. This year's headliners: Lost & Found, Continental Divide, Bluegrass Etc., Copperline, Flint Hill Special, Witcher Brothers, The Tylers. Past performers: Country Gentlemen, The Lonesome River Band, Bluegrass Patriots, Southern Rail, Weary Hearts. Musical competitions, workshops and crafts. Country-Western dancing Saturday night. All performances are held outdoors. Hours: 8:45 a.m.-5 p.m. daily. Seniors (60+) pre-sale: $5 per day. Adults (12-59) pre-sale: $5.50 per day. At gate $6. All children (12 and under) free. A, FF, EF, VF, RF, R, P (on leash), MR, RR, CO, CN, S, RVO, RVN, HN, M

Contact: Barbara Martin, c/o Chamber of Commerce, 201 S. Broadway, Blythe, CA 92225 • Phone: 619-922-8166 • Fax: 619-922-4010

MR = modern restrooms	RR = rustic restrooms	CO = camping on-site	CN = camping nearby	S = hot showers
RVO = RVs on-site	RVN = RVs nearby	HO = hookups on-site	HN = hookups nearby	M = motels nearby

KERN COUNTY BLUEGRASS FESTIVAL AND CRAFT FAIR
May 24-26
Kern County Fairgrounds, Bakersfield, CA

Features a minimum of 6 to 8 bands playing both traditional and progressive bluegrass music. Workshops and crafts area. All performances held indoors. Hours: Friday 5 p.m.-10 p.m., Saturday & Sunday 10 a.m.-6 p.m. Tickets: $5 per day. Children (under 12) free. A, EF, RF, R, MR, CO, S, RVO, HO, M

Contact: Mike Knapp, P.O. Box 7, Lakeshore, CA 93634 • Phone: 209-893-3474 or 209-445-1459 • Fax: 209-893-3474

SUMMER BLUEGRASS FESTIVAL 1996
July 12-14
Traveland USA, Irvine, CA

Since 1995. Annual attendance is 1,000+. Held in a fantastic location with easy freeway access. Free event setup allows for craft demonstrations, musical workshops and seminars. Numerous opportunities for featured jamming. This year's headliners: Alive 'n Pickin', Orange County Bluegrass Band. Folk, traditional and ethnic dancing. All performances held outdoors. Hours: 10-10. Free admission. Free parking. Free RV overnights with refundable deposit (modified dry camp). A, F (full service restaurant on site), R, P, MR, RVO RVN, HN, M

Contact: Peggy Warren or Denise Jimenez, 6441 Burt Road #57, Irvine, CA 92720 • Phone: 714-651-0945 or 800-854-0121 (outside CA) or 800- 432-7227 (outside Orange County) • Fax: 714-552-7056

THE WINTER BLUEGRASS FESTIVAL & CONFERENCE ON WESTERN BLUEGRASS
February 8-11
LeBaron Hotel, San Jose, CA

This is the first year for this 5-day celebration of bluegrass music. It includes an extensive conference on western bluegrass which will be attended by major figures in the bluegrass arena. This year's headliners: IIIrd Tyme Out, Lonesome River Band, Dry Branch Fire Squad, Lynn Morris Band. All performances are held indoors. Workshops, children's activities and crafts. Hours: 10 a.m.-midnight. Tickets: $60 early bird, with gradual increases closer to the festival; $75 at the gate. A, F (restaurants in hotel), R, CC, MR, M (this event is held in a hotel)

Contact: Fred Morris, Winter Bluegrass Festival, P.O. Box 31557, San Francisco, CA 94131 • Phone: 415-585-8234 • Fax: same (call first)

A = wheelchair accessible   I = interpreter for hearing impaired   F = food   FF = fast food   EF = ethnic food
VF = vegetarian food   RF = regional food   R = restaurants nearby   P = pets welcome   CC = credit cards

Colorado

1996 Seventh Annual Bluegrass on the River
May 31-June 2
Greenway & Nature Center, Pueblo, CO

Since 1989. Annual attendance is 5,000. Features bluegrass, bluegrass, bluegrass for 33 glorious non-stop hours. Held on the banks of the beautiful Arkansas River, shaded by big cottonwood trees, the staff of the Greenway & Nature Center of Pueblo presents natural history programs for young and old. The picturesque surroundings provide an extraordinary setting for the festival. The Pickin' Parlor offers the authentic way to enjoy bluegrass music — live, in person, no microphones, just true, acoustic sound. Another unique event is the "band scramble," a lively and fun musical competition. Watch the exciting Colorado Clogging Shootout, a competitive traditional dance show with the top performers from the Rocky Mountain region. Like bluegrass music, this high energy, spirited art form with jigs, reels, and flings is uniquely American. Tap your toes and stomp your feet to "bluegrass boogie music" at the Saturday Night Dance. Past headliners: Bluegrass Patriots, Echo Creek, String Fever, Pete & Joan Wernick, Cow Town Boogie, and more. Performances held both indoors and outdoors with an outdoor covered area for the audience. No alcohol allowed on site. Opens for camping Friday at noon. Saturday and Sunday hours 10 a.m.-6 p.m. Prices: $10 weekend / $6 day. Children (7-11) $2 / day. Children 6 and under free. A, I (some performances), FF, EF, VF, RF, R, MR, RR, CO, CN, S, RVO, RVN, HN, M

Contact: Timothy Sandmark, Greenway & Nature Center, 5200 Nature Center Road, Pueblo, CO 81003 • Phone: 719-545-9114 • Fax: 719-545-3484

Boulder Folk and Bluegrass Festival
July 13
Chautauqua Park, Boulder, CO

Since 1983. Annual attendance is 1,000. Features international and traditional folk, new folk and bluegrass. Distinguished by its small, intimate, "livingroom-style" workshops. Held in a lovely, historic section of Boulder right at the foothills in a beautiful park setting. Guests can stay in cabins in the park, where there is also an excellent restaurant. Past headliners include Arlo Guthrie, Bela Fleck, Shawn Colvin, Hot Tuna, Ferron, Tom Rush, Doc Watson, Beausoleil. All performances are held indoors. Hours are noon-11 p.m. Tickets are $17 to $22. Advance tickets are available. A, R, CC, MR, M

Contact: Nona Gandelman, P.O. Box 970, Boulder, CO 80306 • Phone: 303-443-5858 • Fax: 303-443-5894

MR = modern restrooms   RR = rustic restrooms   CO = camping on-site   CN = camping nearby   S = hot showers
RVO = RVs on-site   RVN = RVs nearby   HO = hookups on-site   HN = hookups nearby   M = motels nearby

Colorado Mid-Winter Bluegrass Festival
February 16-18
Holiday Inn – Plaza Inn, Fort Collins, CO

> Since 1986. Annual attendance is 1,500. Music is 90% bluegrass, 10% folk and jazz. Features poolside jam sessions 'round the clock. Three stages with great jamming. Hosts the world's only "under-water banjo contest." This year's headliners: Osborne Brothers, Bluegrass Patriots, and 15 other acts. Past performers: Doyle Lawson, Rose Maddox, Tim & Molly O'Brian, Front Range, Peter Rowan, Del McCoury. Musical competitions, workshops, children's activities. All performances held indoors. Hours: 10 a.m.-11 a.m. daily. Saturday $20, Friday and Sunday $15 per day. Three-day pass in advance is $35. Pass for Saturday and Sunday is $30. Advance ticket sales available. F (full restaurant), FF, R, MR, S, M

> Contact: Ken Seaman, 1807 Essex Drive, Ft. Collins, CO 80526 • Phone: 907-482-0863

Rocky Grass – The Rocky Mountain Bluegrass Festival
August 2-4
Festival Site, Lyons, CO

> Since 1972. Annual attendance is 3,000. Held at a beautiful site with a river and on-site camping. Incredible pickin' at campground and the very best bluegrass music. Past performers: Seldom Scene, Jim & Jesse, Doc Watson, Del McCoury, Alison Krauss, Jimmy Martin, Tony Rice, and many more. Musical competitions, workshops, children's activities and crafts area. All performances held outdoors. A covered area is available for the audience. Hours: Friday evening and all day Saturday and Sunday. Tentative ticket prices: $55 for 3 days, $75 for camping and 3-day pass, $20 for Friday, $25 for Saturday, $25 for Sunday. Advance ticket sales available. A, FF, EF, VF, RF, R, RR, CO, CN, S, RVO, RVN, M

> Contact: Craig, Sally or Jo, Planet Bluegrass, 500 West Main, Lyons, CO 80540 • Phone: 800-624-2422 or 303-449-6007 • Fax: 303-823-0849

Telluride Bluegrass Festival
June (call for exact dates)
Town Park, Telluride, CO

> Since 1973. Annual attendance is 8,000 to 10,000. This four-day festival features an incredible mix of outstanding music (bluegrass, folk, country and others) held at what the organizers describe as "the most beautiful setting on Earth!" Awesome scenery surrounds the audience while the finest musicians play. Past performers: Mary Chapin Carpenter, James Taylor, Del McCoury Band, Paco deLucia, Bela Fleck & The Flecktones, Sam Bush, and many, many more. Musical competitions, workshops, children's activities, and crafts area. All performances held outdoors. Hours: 10 a.m.-11 p.m. daily. Tickets: early bird approx. $95 for 4 days; at the gate

---

A = wheelchair accessible   I = interpreter for hearing impaired   F = food   FF = fast food   EF = ethnic food
VF = vegetarian food   RF = regional food   R = restaurants nearby   P = pets welcome   CC = credit cards

around $115 for 4 days. Daily prices: Thursday $25-$30, Friday $30-$35, Saturday and Sunday $35-$40. Discounts offered on ticket orders placed before February 1st. A, FF, EF, VF, RF, R, CC, RR, CO, CN, S, RVO, RVN, HO, HN, M (hotels)

Contact: Craig, Sally or Jo, Planet Bluegrass, 500 West Main, Lyons, CO 80540 • Phone: 800-624-2422 or 303-449-6007 • Fax: 303-823-0849

Connecticut

CONNECTICUT FAMILY FOLK FESTIVAL

July 27-28
Elizabeth Park, Hartford, CT

Since 1974. Annual attendance is 800. Features folk and bluegrass music with the aim of educating families about these musical genres. This year's headliners: Sandy & Caroline Paton, Ron Renniger. Past performers: Bill Staines, Fred Small. All performances held outdoors. Music related workshops. Hours: 27th noon-8:30 p.m.; 28th noon-5:30 p.m. Admission is FREE to all events. A, FF, R, MR, M

Contact: Len Domler, Connecticut Family Folk Festival, 14 Southwood Road, Cromwell, CT 06416 • Phone: 860-632-7547

Delaware

EASTERN SHORE BLUEGRASS ASSOCIATION
16TH ANNUAL FESTIVAL

June 14-16
Delaware State Fairgrounds, Rt. 13 South, Harrington, DE

Since 1981. Annual attendance is 2,000. This family-style festival has supervised children's programs, easy access (paved roads), and is held in a level, grassy location with some wooded areas. This year's headliners: Lonesome River Band, Boys From Indiana, Sand Mountain Boys, Gary Ferguson Band, Jerry McCoury, Bob Paisley, and others. Past performers include Osborne Brothers, Jim & Jesse, Mac Wiseman, Larry Sparks, Bluegrass Cardinals, Country Gentlemen, Bill Harrell. Musical competitions. Crafts area. All performances held outdoors. A covered area is available for the audience. Hours: Friday 6 p.m.-midnight, Saturday noon-11 p.m., Sunday 10 a.m.-5 p.m. Tickets: weekend advance $32, at gate $40. Friday $15, Saturday $20, Sunday $12. Children (12 and under) free. Senior citizen and student discounts. A, FF, RF, R, P (on leash; not in concert area), MR, CO, S, RVO, RVN, HO, HN, M

Contact: Ray Lewis, P.O. Box 525, Wyoming, DE 19934 • Phone: 302-492-1048

MR = modern restrooms   RR = rustic restrooms   CO = camping on-site   CN = camping nearby   S = hot showers
RVO = RVs on-site   RVN = RVs nearby   HO = hookups on-site   HN = hookups nearby   M = motels nearby

Florida

1996 KISSIMMEE KIWANIS BLUEGRASS FESTIVAL
March 7-10
Silver Spurs Rodeo Grounds, Kissimmee, FL

Since 1977. Annual attendance is 5,000. This nineteen year old festival features traditional American music for the whole family encompassing bluegrass, country, Western swing, and Cajun. This year's headliners are The Osborne Brothers and The Lewis Family. Past performers include Del McCoury, Bill Harrell, and Jim & Jesse. Workshops and crafts area. All performances held outdoors. A covered area is available for the audience. Hours are Thursday 4 p.m.-midnight, Friday 3 p.m.-midnight, Saturday 11 a.m.-midnight, Sunday 10 a.m.-2 p.m. Ticket prices: Thursday $10.75, Friday $12.75, Saturday $18.25, Sunday $16. Four-day pass at gate $53.50, in advance (by 12/1/95) $48.25. Three-day pass at gate $46, in advance (by 12/1/95) $39.50. Admission for children under 16 is free. A, FF, RF, R, P (on leash; not in concert area), CC, RR, CO, CN, RVO, RVN, HN, M

Contact: Kissimmee Bluegrass Festival, American Bluegrass Network, P.O. Box 456, Orlando, FL 32802 • Phone: 800-473-7773 or 407-856-0245 • Fax: 407-858-0007

ANNUAL SUNSHINE STATE BLUEGRASS FESTIVAL
March 14-17
Harbor Front Laishley Park, Punta Gorda, FL

Since 1988. Annual attendance is tens of thousands. This is the largest bluegrass festival in the South. Features bluegrass and traditional country music. Past performers: Jim & Jesse, Mac Wiseman, Chubby Wise, Boys from Indiana, James King, Sand Mountain Boys, U.S. Navy Band, and many, many more. Children's activities, crafts area, and Sanctioned National Clogging Championship Competition. All performances held outdoors. Hours: 9 a.m.-11 p.m. daily. Tickets: $5 per day, $20 weekend. Pass required for free camping. Advance ticket sales available. A, F, R, MR, RR, RVO, RVN, HN, M

Contact: Bill Pattie, Annual Sunshine State Bluegrass Festival, P.O. Box 372, Punta Gorda, FL 33951-0372 • Phone: 941-639-3646 • Fax: 941-639-5966

BLUEGRASS MUSIC FESTIVAL
April 11-14
Spirit of the Suwannee Park, Live Oak, FL

Since 1986. Annual attendance is 3,000. Features bluegrass music in a beautiful tree-shaded amphitheatre terraced for folding chair seating. Many walking trails, swimming pool. Old-time farm machinery museum. This year's headliners: IIIrd

---

A = wheelchair accessible   I = interpreter for hearing impaired   F = food   FF = fast food   EF = ethnic food
VF = vegetarian food   RF = regional food   R = restaurants nearby   P = pets welcome   CC = credit cards

Tyme Out, Chubby Wise. Past performers: Alison Krauss, Doyle Lawson, Lewis Family, Seldom Scene, Dry Branch Fire Squad. Performances held both indoors and outdoors. Workshops, children's activities, and crafts area. Afternoon and evening shows. Tickets: approx. $25-$30 for the weekend. Advance ticket sales available. A, FF, R, MR, CO, CN, RVO, RVN, HO, HN, M

Contact: Jean Cornett, Bluegrass Music Festival, Rt. 1, Box 98, Live Oak, FL 32060 • Phone: 904-364-1683 • Fax: 904-364-2998

BLUEGRASS MUSIC IN THE FALL
October 24-26
Spirit of the Suwannee Park, Live Oak, FL

Since 1986. Annual attendance is 4,000. Features traditional bluegrass music. With the concerts there will be work sessions with the bands. Past performers: Doyle Lawson, Ralph Stanley, Traditional Grass, etc. Children's activities and crafts area. Also a haunted house, pumpkin carving and costume judging. Performances and events held both indoors and outdoors. Held in the afternoon and evening. Tickets: $20 to $25. Advance ticket sales available. A, FF, RF, R, CC, MR, CO, CN, RVO, RVN, HO, HN, M

Contact: Jean Cornett, Fall Bluegrass Festival, Rt. 1, Box 98, Live Oak, FL 32060 • Phone: 904-364-1683 • Fax: 904-364-2998

DIXIELAND BLUEGRASS FAMILY REUNION
February 16-18, May 17-19, October 18-20
Dixieland Music Park, Hwy. 301, Waldo, FL

Since 1988. This is a family-owned festival which strives for personal contact with each fan. Three flea markets and fishing within walking distance. Easy, accessible accommodations. This year's headliners: Jim & Jessie, Boyd Brothers, Larkin Family, Bass Mountain. Past performers: Bill Monroe, Ralph Stanley, Gov. Jimmy Davis, Roni Stoneman, Mac Wiseman, Sand Mountain. Workshops, crafts area, and clogging. Performances are both indoors and outdoors. A covered area is available for the audience outdoors. "25 hour" restaurant. Hours: Friday 6 p.m.–11 p.m., Saturday noon-11 p.m., Sunday 10 a.m.-2 p.m. Weekend rate: $25. Friday $12, Saturday $16, Sunday $8. Kids (16 and under) free. A, F, R, P, MR, S, RVO, RVN, HO, HN, M

Contact: Sheila Stanford, Rt. 1, Box 244, Waldo, FL 32694 • Phone: 904-468-2622 (after 9 p.m.)

MR = modern restrooms   RR = rustic restrooms   CO = camping on-site   CN = camping nearby   S = hot showers
RVO = RVs on-site   RVN = RVs nearby   HO = hookups on-site   HN = hookups nearby   M = motels nearby

DIXIELAND BLUEGRASS MONTHLY "PICKIN & GRININ"

Jan. 12-13, Feb. 9-10, Mar. 8-9, Apr. 12-13, May 10-11, Jun. 7-8,
Jul. 12-13, Aug. 9-10, Sep. 13-14, Oct. 11-12, Nov. 8-9, Dec. 13-14
(the second Friday and Saturday of each month)
Dixieland Music Park, Hwy. 301, Waldo, FL

Since 1988. This monthly "pickin and grinin" is an informal event which gives everyone opportunities to play together from beginners to professionals. "25 hour" restaurant. All events held indoors. Admission is free. A, F, R, P, MR, S, RVO, RVN, HO, HN, M

Contact: Sheila Stanford, Rt. 1, Box 244, Waldo, FL 32694 • Phone: 904-468-2622 (after 9 p.m.)

EVERGLADES BLUEGRASS CONVENTION

February 9-11
Ives Estates Optimist Grounds, N.E. 15 Avenue & Ives Dairy Rd.
North Miami Beach, FL

Since 1977. Great bluegrass music in the middle of winter — no snow! This year's headliners: Osborne Brothers, Chubby Wise, Cox Family, Clark Family, Ramblin' Rose Band, Redwing & local bands. Past performers: Bass Mountain, Johnson Mountain Boys, Boys From Indiana, Ralph Stanley, Bluegrass Cardinals, Raymond Fairchild. Crafts and traditional dancing. Hours: Friday 6 p.m.-midnight, Saturday 10 a.m.-midnight, Sunday 10 a.m.-4:30 p.m. Advance weekend tickets $24, at gate $27. Friday only $8, Saturday only $15, Sunday only $8. Children 13-16 pay 1/2 price with adult. Children under 12 free. A, F, R, P (not in concert area), MR, CO, CN, S, RVN, M

Contact: James Mason, 3330 S.W. 37th Street, Hollywood, FL 33023 • Phone: 305-983-8164

FLORIDA'S WITHLACOOCHEE RIVER BLUEGRASS JAMBOREE

March 29-31, October 31-November 2
Withlacoochee Bluegrass Park, 6 mi. west, Hwy. 40 W., Dunnellon, FL

Since 1980. Provides a unique river bank atmosphere at the historic site of an old steamboat landing. Good clean family-oriented fun and the best bluegrass bands on the circuit. Past performers: Bill Monroe, Chubby Wise, Jerry Clower, Little Jimmy Dickens, Jim & Jesse, Lewis Family, Larry Stephenson, Lonesome Standard Time, Goins Brothers, Grandpa Jones, Osborne Brothers, Peter Rowan, J.D. Crowe, Ralph Stanley. All performances held outdoors. A covered area is available for the audience. Crafts area. Hours: Friday & Saturday 1:00 p.m.-midnight, Sunday 10 a.m.-4 p.m. Tickets: $29 advance (all three days); $32 at the gate (all three days). FF, RF, R, P (not in concert area), MR, RR, CO, CN, S, RVO, RVN, HO, HN, M

Contact: Lonnie Knight, P.O. Box 180, Dunnellon, FL 34430 • Phone: 904-489-8330

A = wheelchair accessible   I = interpreter for hearing impaired   F = food   FF = fast food   EF = ethnic food
VF = vegetarian food   RF = regional food   R = restaurants nearby   P = pets welcome   CC = credit cards

Gulf Coast Bluegrass Music Assoc. Spring Festival
May 9-11
Holiday Hills Bluegrass Park, Laurel Hill, FL

Since 1983. Annual attendance is 1,300. This festival features bluegrass and gospel music in a beautiful, well-kept campground setting with top facilities. The attendees have been coming for many years so it feels like a family reunion. Quality entertainment, craft vendors, hot food concessions, demos, and many educational and entertaining events are scheduled. This year's headliners: IIIrd Tyme Out, Larkin Family, New Tradition, Larry Stephenson and others. Past performers: Larry Sparks, Stevens Family, Jerry & Tammy Sullivan, Texas Winds, Liberty, Cedar Creek, and many, many more. All performances held outdoors. A covered stage and pavilion are available – the show goes on rain or shine. The park opens for campers May 5. Tickets: weekend $18, Thursday night only $5, Friday night only $8, Saturday (all day and night) $12, Saturday night (after 5 p.m.) $8, children under with parents admitted free. Rough camping free with weekend ticket. W/E hookups $8 per night. A, F (BBQ, breakfasts, dinners, ice cream), FF, R (10 mi.), P (on leash), MR, S, RVO, HO, M

Contact: Cheryl Copeland, Secretary, 3240 Green Valley Drive, Pensacola, FL 32526 • Phone: 904-944-1885 or 904-994-7367

Gulf Coast Bluegrass Music Assoc. Fall Festival
August 29-31
Holiday Hills Bluegrass Park, Laurel Hill, FL

Since 1983. Annual attendance is 1,300. This festival features bluegrass and gospel music in a beautiful, well-kept campground setting with top facilities. The attendees have been coming for many years so it feels like a family reunion. Quality entertainment, craft vendors, hot food concessions, demos, and many educational and entertaining events are scheduled. Past performers: Larry Sparks, Stevens Family, Jerry & Tammy Sullivan, Texas Winds, Liberty, Cedar Creek, and many, many more. All performances held outdoors. A covered stage and pavilion are available – the show goes on rain or shine. The park opens for campers August 25. Tickets: weekend $18, Thursday night only $5, Friday night only $8, Saturday (all day and night) $12, Saturday night (after 5 p.m.) $8, children under with parents admitted free. Rough camping free with weekend ticket. W/E hookups $8 per night. A, F (BBQ, breakfasts, dinners, ice cream), FF, R (10 mi.), P (on leash), MR, S, RVO, HO, M

Contact: Cheryl Copeland, Secretary, 3240 Green Valley Drive, Pensacola, FL 32526 • Phone: 904-944-1885 or 904-994-7367

Labor Day Weekend
August 30-September 2
Spirit of the Suwannee Park, Live Oak, FL

Since 1989. Features bluegrass music in a beautiful tree-shaded amphitheatre terraced for folding chair seating. Children's activities, old-tyme games, boiled

---

MR = modern restrooms   RR = rustic restrooms   CO = camping on-site   CN = camping nearby   S = hot showers
RVO = RVs on-site   RVN = RVs nearby   HO = hookups on-site   HN = hookups nearby   M = motels nearby

peanuts. Bluegrass pickin' Saturday night. Hours vary. Admission is FREE; fee for camping. A, F, R, MR, RR, CO, CN, RVO, RVN, HO, HN, M

Contact: Jean Cornett, Labor Day Weekend, Rt. 1, Box 98, Live Oak, FL 32060 • Phone: 904-364-1683 • Fax: 904-364-2998

LIVELY LIBERTY FESTIVITIES

July 4-7
Spirit of the Suwannee Park, Live Oak, FL

Since 1989. Features bluegrass and country-western music in a beautiful tree-shaded amphitheatre terraced for folding chair seating. Children's activities and fireworks. Bluegrass pickin' Saturday night. Hours vary. Admission is FREE; fee for camping. A, F, R, MR, RR, CO, CN, RVO, RVN, HO, HN, M

Contact: Jean Cornett, Lively Liberty Festivities, Rt. 1, Box 98, Live Oak, FL 32060 • Phone: 904-364-1683 • Fax: 904-364-2998

MEMORIAL DAY WEEKEND

May 24-27
Spirit of the Suwannee Park, Live Oak, FL

Since 1989. Features bluegrass music in a beautiful tree-shaded amphitheatre terraced for folding chair seating. Children's activities. Bluegrass pickin' Saturday night. Hours vary. Admission is FREE; fee for camping. A, F, R, MR, RR, CO, CN, RVO, RVN, HO, HN, M

Contact: Jean Cornett, Memorial Day Weekend, Rt. 1, Box 98, Live Oak, FL 32060 • Phone: 904-364-1683 • Fax: 904-364-2998

NEW STAR RISING

November 21-24
Spirit of the Suwannee Park, Live Oak, FL

Since 1990. Annual attendance is 1,500. This is a festival for young bands. There are plenty of workshops for beginners and lots of parking lot picking. Past performers: Redwing, Paul Adkins, Laura Lewis, Brushfire. Family and children's activities, crafts area, and dancing (clogging and traditional). Performances held both indoors and outdoors. Hobo stew, soup, beans and cornbread. Hours: Thursday evening, Friday and Saturday afternoon and evening, Sunday morning. Tentative ticket pricing: $18 for 4 days (call to confirm). Advance ticket sales available. A, FF, R, P (camping area only), CC, MR, CO, RVO, RVN, HO, HN, M

Contact: Jean Cornett, New Star Rising, Rt. 1, Box 98, Live Oak, FL 32060 • Phone: 904-364-1683 • Fax: 904-364-2998

A = wheelchair accessible   I = interpreter for hearing impaired   F = food   FF = fast food   EF = ethnic food
VF = vegetarian food   RF = regional food   R = restaurants nearby   P = pets welcome   CC = credit cards

SUMMER SWAMP STOMP

July (call for exact date)
Tallahassee Museum of History & Natural Science, Tallahassee, FL

Since 1983. Annual attendance is 1,000. Summer Swamp Stomp offers a unique combination of music, dancing and storytelling. Included in the ticket price is access to a 52 acre museum complete with exhibit gallery, historical buildings, native Florida animals, hands-on science center, farm and nature trail. Features bluegrass, traditional, folk and acoustical music. Past performers: Del Suggs, Pierce Pettice, Sandy Creek Stringers, and Dead Reckoning. Children's activities. All performances held outdoors. Hours are 1 p.m.–5 p.m. Adults are $5, seniors $4, children $3, children 3 and under free, and museum members are free. A, FF, VF, R, MR, RVN, HN, M

Contact: Janet R. Borneman, Festival Director, 3945 Museum Drive, Tallahassee, FL 32310 • Phone: 904-575-8684 • Fax: 904-574-8243

TATER HILL REUNION

February 16-18
DeSoto County Fairgrounds, Arcadia, FL

Since 1987. Annual attendance is 6,000. Features bluegrass, country and gospel music (Sunday a.m.) in a hometown, family atmosphere. All proceeds benefit Special Olympics! Crafts area. Hours: Friday and Saturday 10 a.m.–11 p.m., Sunday 10 a.m.–6 p.m. Tickets: Weekend pass $10 per person; daily rate $6 per person. Camping on grounds free; no hookups. Advance ticket sales available. A, FF, RF, R, P (on leash), MR, CO, RVN, HN, M

Contact: Jerry or Betty Porter, Tater Hill Reunion, 2789 S.W. County Road 769, Arcadia, FL 33821 • Phone: 941-993-1473

THANKSGIVING HARVEST WEEKEND

November 28-December 1
Spirit of the Suwannee Park, Live Oak, FL

Since 1988. Annual attendance is 1,000. Features bluegrass music, fly wheelers demonstrations, antique tractor pull, old-tyme farm equipment demonstrations, cane syrup tasting swamp cabbage samples, yesteryear's trades, mule wagon rides. Bluegrass pickin' Saturday night. Performances held both indoors and outdoors. Hours vary. No charge for activities except concert which is $5. A, F, R, CC, MR, RR, CO, S, CN, RVO, HO, M

Contact: Jean Cornett, Thanksgiving Harvest Weekend, Rt. 1, Box 98, Live Oak, FL 32060 • Phone: 904-364-1683 • Fax: 904-364-2998

MR = modern restrooms   RR = rustic restrooms   CO = camping on-site   CN = camping nearby   S = hot showers
RVO = RVs on-site   RVN = RVs nearby   HO = hookups on-site   HN = hookups nearby   M = motels nearby

Yee Haw Junction Bluegrass Festival
January 18–21
Behind the Historic Desert Inn, Yee Haw Junction, FL

Since 1995. Annual attendance is 5,000 to 7,000. A family-reunion type atmosphere with wonderful people who provide a rare, friendly presence. This year's headliners: The Prospectors, Gilbert Hancock, Kevin Williamson & Shadowridge, Bass Mountain Boys, Chubby Wise, James Rogers. Past performers: Doyle Lawson & Quicksilver, South Ocean String Band, Gilbert Hancock, Chubby Wise, The Prospectors. All performances held outdoors. A covered area is available for the audience. Musical competitions and crafts area. Hours: 10 a.m.–11 p.m. Tickets: $26 for 4 days ($23 advance), $23 for 3 days ($20 advance), $8 per day. F (hot meals), FF, P, CC, RR, CO, CN, M

Contact: Davina Mathews, Ben Roberts or Penny Murphy, 606 N. Ingraham Avenue, Lakeland, FL 33801 • Phone: 941-687-8993 or 800-329-8993 • Fax: 941-686-1950

Georgia

22nd Annual Dahlonega Bluegrass Festival
June 20–22
Blackburn Park & Campground, Dahlonega, GA

Since 1974. Family entertainment and top bluegrass bands. Past performers: Bill Monroe, Osborne Brothers, Jim & Jesse, Lewis Family. All performances held outdoors. A covered area is available for the audience. Crafts area. Hours: noon–11 p.m. daily. Call for ticket information. Advance ticket sales available. A, FF, R, CC, MR, RR, CO, CN, S, RVO, RVN, HO, HN, M

Contact: Norman Adams or Tony Anderson, P.O. Box 98, 112 N. Park Street, Dahlonega, GA 30533 • Phone: 706-864-7203 • Fax: 706-864-1037

9th Annual Lewis Family Homecoming & Bluegrass Festival
May 2–4
Elijah Clark State Park, Lincolnton, GA

Since 1987. Family entertainment and top bluegrass bands. Past performers: Bill Monroe, Osborne Brothers, Jim & Jesse, Lewis Family. All performances held outdoors. A covered area is available for the audience. Crafts area. Hours: noon–11 p.m. daily. Call for ticket information. Advance ticket sales available. A, FF, R, CC, MR, S, RVO, RVN, HO, HN, M

Contact: Norman Adams or Tony Anderson, P.O. Box 98, 112 N. Park Street, Dahlonega, GA 30533 • Phone: 706-864-7203 • Fax: 706-864-1037

A = wheelchair accessible I = interpreter for hearing impaired F = food FF = fast food EF = ethnic food
VF = vegetarian food RF = regional food R = restaurants nearby P = pets welcome CC = credit cards

GEORGIA MOUNTAIN FAIR
August 7-18
Georgia Mountain Fairgrounds, Hiawassee, GA

Since 1951. Annual attendance is 125,000. This is a non-commercial fair, with entertainment designed to appeal to all ages. Arts & crafts, "ole-timey" Pioneer Village, exhibits, rides and games. Country music performed by Nashville talent and locals. Clogging. Past performers include Jerry Reed, Jerry Clower, Connie Smith, T. Graham Grown, Merle Haggard, Sawyer Brown, Joe Diffie, Mark Chesnutt. Performances held both indoors and outdoors. A covered area is available for the audience outdoors. Hours: Monday-Thursday 10 a.m.-9 p.m., Saturday 10 a.m.-10 p.m., Sunday 10 a.m.-6 p.m. Tickets: $6 for adults; children (under 10) free. Advance ticket sales available. A, FF, EF, VF, RF, R, CC, MR, S, RVO, RVN, HO, HN, M

Contact: Hilda Thomason, Georgia Mountain Fair, Box 444, Hiawassee, GA 30546 • Phone: 706-896-4191 • Fax: 706-896-4209

HAMBY MOUNTAIN 16TH ANNUAL FALL BLUEGRASS FESTIVAL
September 26-28
Hamby Mountain Music Park, Baldwin, GA

Since 1980. Annual attendance is 300±. Features local and national bluegrass bands. This year's headliners: Jim & Jessie, The Virginia Boys, Gains Brothers, Lewis Family, Wildwood Girls, and 10 other bands. Thursday 6 p.m.-11:30 p.m., Friday 2 p.m.-11:30 p.m., Saturday noon-11:30 p.m. Three-day advance tickets $30, at the gate $39. Thursday $10, Friday $12, Saturday $15. After 8 p.m. on Saturday $12. A, FF, RF, R, P (not in concert area), MR, S, RVO, RVN, HO, HN, M

Contact: Charles Hamby, Fall Bluegrass Festival, P.O. Box 851, Seneca, SC 29679 • Phone: 803-972-9498

HAMBY MOUNTAIN 16TH ANNUAL SPRING BLUEGRASS FESTIVAL
May 30-June 1
Hamby Mountain Music Park, Baldwin, GA

Since 1980. Annual attendance is 300±. Features local and national bluegrass bands. This year's headliners: Ralph Stanley, Clark Family, Sand Mountain Boys, Stevens Family, Curtis Blackwell & Dixie Bluegrass, and 9 other bands. Thursday 6 p.m.-11:30 p.m., Friday 2 p.m.-11:30 p.m., Saturday noon-11:30 p.m. Three-day advance tickets $30, at the gate $39. Thursday $10, Friday $12, Saturday $15. After 8 p.m. on Saturday $12. A, FF, RF, R, P (not in concert area), MR, S, RVO, RVN, HO, HN, M

Contact: Charles Hamby, Spring Bluegrass Festival, P.O. Box 851, Seneca, SC 29679 • Phone: 803-972-9498

MR = modern restrooms   RR = rustic restrooms   CO = camping on-site   CN = camping nearby   S = hot showers
RVO = RVs on-site   RVN = RVs nearby   HO = hookups on-site   HN = hookups nearby   M = motels nearby

HILLSIDE BLUEGRASS FESTIVAL
September 21-23
Hillside Bluegrass Park, Cochran, GA

Since 1992. This family-oriented festival has lots of parking lot pickin'. This year's headliners: Jim & Jesse, The Virginia Boys, The Gillis Brothers, Charlie Waller & The Country Gentlemen. Past performers: Ralph Stanley, The Lewis Family, Charlie Cline. Workshops and crafts area. All performances held outdoors. A covered area is available for the audience. Hours: Thursday 8-??, Friday 6:30-??, Saturday 11-??. Tickets: $20 for the weekend (3 days); Saturday only $10, Friday only $8. Advance ticket sales available. A (limited), FF (home cooked), R, P (on leash), MR, S, RVO, HO, M

Contact: Van or Jean Holland, Hillside Bluegrass Festival, Rt. 5, Box 41, Cochran, GA 31014 • Phone: 912-934-6694

RIVERWALK BLUEGRASS FESTIVAL
May 25
Riverwalk Amphitheatre, Augusta, GA

Since 1989. Annual attendance is 1,400. This family-oriented concert event features bluegrass, acoustic and gospel music in an amphitheater overlooking the beautiful Savannah River. It is within walking distance of the Radisson Hotel. Past headliners: Alison Krauss, J.D. Crowe, Cox Family, Avalanche, Live Wire. Children's activities and crafts. All performances are held outdoors. Hours: 4 p.m.-10 p.m. Price: $10. Advance ticket sales available. A, F, R, CC, MR, M

Contact: Doug Flowers or Jeff Synan, P.O. Box 31117, Augusta, GA 30903 • Phone: 706-592-0054 or 706-868-8726

SUGAR CREEK BLUEGRASS FESTIVAL
June 7-9, July 26-28, October 11-13
Sugar Creek Music Park & Campground, Blue Ridge, GA

Since 1978. Features bluegrass and country music. Past performers: Ralph Stanley, The Gillis Brothers, Southern Breeze, Bill Grant & Delia Bell, Earl Bull & Dusty Valley. Thursday night jam session. Guests are requested to bring a covered dish. Friday 6 p.m. to ??, Saturday 12-12. Tickets: $12 Friday, $14 Saturday. Children (under 6) free. A, F, R, P (on leash), RR, CO, RVO, RVN, HO, HN, M

Contact: Vida Cox, Sugar Creek Bluegrass Festival, 1220 Cox Road, Blue Ridge, GA 30513 • Phone: 706-632-2560

A = wheelchair accessible   I = interpreter for hearing impaired   F = food   FF = fast food   EF = ethnic food
VF = vegetarian food   RF = regional food   R = restaurants nearby   P = pets welcome   CC = credit cards

TWIN OAKS PARK BLUEGRASS CONVENTION
May 3-4, September 6-7
Twin Oaks Park, Hoboken, GA

Since 1975. Annual attendance is 6,000. Past performers include Liberty Bluegrass. Crafts area and clogging. All performances are held outdoors. There is a covered area for the audience. Hours are Friday 7:30 p.m.-midnight, Saturday 1 p.m.-midnight. Tickets are $6 Friday, $7 Saturday. A, FF, R, P (on leash), MR, RVO, HO, M

Contact: Ira W. Crews, Rt. 1, Box 115, Hoboken, GA 31542 • Phone: 912-458-2365

Idaho

NATIONAL OLDTIME FIDDLERS' CONTEST
June 19-24
Weiser High School, Weiser, ID

Since 1953. Annual attendance is 20,000. Over 350 of the top fiddlers in the world compete in Weiser for over $23,000 in trophies and prize money. Competitors range from ages 3 to 93. The competition is mixed with some of the best country bands in the U.S. Jamming can be found 24-hours-a-day in the campgrounds, parks and hospitality centers. It's a week-long celebration with nonstop activities – jam sessions, a parade, and historic fiddle mementos, which all help preserve the old time music and atmosphere. There's a carnival, arts & crafts, and enough to fill anyone's photo album and thrill any fiddle fan. All contests are held in the air-conditioned Weiser High School Gymnasium. Contesting runs 8 a.m.-11 p.m. Monday through Friday and Saturday 6 p.m.-11 p.m. Past headliners include Buck Owens, Jana Jae, Grammy award-winner Mark O'Connor, The Bullas, Boohers, Fiddle Across America. Workshops, children's activities and clog dancing. Ticket prices vary from $6 to $12. Seniors are free 8 a.m.-5 p.m. Friday. Advance ticket sales are available. A, F, R, P (not in contest area), CC, MR, CN, S, RVO, RVN, HN, M

Contact: Layna Hafer, Contest Director, 8 East Idaho, Weiser, ID 83672 • Phone: 208-549-0450 or 800-437-1280 • Fax: 208-549-0450

MR = modern restrooms   RR = rustic restrooms   CO = camping on-site   CN = camping nearby   S = hot showers
RVO = RVs on-site   RVN = RVs nearby   HO = hookups on-site   HN = hookups nearby   M = motels nearby

Illinois

Greater Downstate Indoor Bluegrass Festival & Guitar Show
November 8-10
Holiday Inn Conference Hotel, I-72 exit 133A, Decatur, IL

Since 1988. Annual attendance is 4,500. This is Illinois' largest indoor bluegrass festival and vintage guitar show. Held at a terrific convention hotel, this is an "under roof" family festival. This year's headliners: Osborne Brothers, Dry Branch Fire Squad, IIIrd Tyme Out, New Coon Creek Girls, Clair Lynch, Rarely Herd, and 6 other bands. Past performers: Jim & Jesse, Ralph Stanley, Doyle Lawson & Quicksilver, Cox Family, Rhonda Vincent, Front Range, Lynn Morris. Musical competitions, workshops, children's activities, and crafts area. Hours: Friday 2:30 p.m. through Sunday 4 p.m. Weekend pass is $25. Per day rate is $10 and up. Children admitted at half price. Advance ticket sales available. A, F (full service on site), MR, S, M (festival held at hotel)

Contact: Terry M. Lease, Downstate Illinois Bluegrass Assoc., P.O. Box 456, Jacksonville, IL 62651 • Phone: 217-243-3159

Northern Illinois in Naperville Bluegrass Festival
March 8-10
Holiday Inn, Naperville, IL

Since 1995. Expected attendance is 2,500. A great family-oriented bluegrass festival with a fiddle contest. This year's headliners: Eddie Adcock Band, Cox Family, Jim & Jesse, Special Consensus, Rarely Herd, and 10 other bands. Past performers: Ralph Stanley. Musical competitions (fiddle contest), workshops, children's activities, and crafts area. All performances held indoors. Hours: Friday 7:30 p.m. through Sunday 3:30 p.m. Weekend pass is $25. Per day is $10 and up. Children admitted half price. Advance ticket sales available. A, F (full service on site), R, MR, S, M (festival held at motor lodge)

Contact: Terry M. Lease, Downstate Illinois Bluegrass Assoc., P.O. Box 456, Jacksonville, IL 62651 • Phone: 217-243-3159

Rockome Gardens Bluegrass Festival
August 17-18
Rockome Gardens, 5 mi. west Arcola on Rt. 133, Arcola, IL

Since 1992. Annual attendance is 3,500. An outstanding family festival held in a unique setting in the heart of Illinois' Amish country. Nationally-known groups will headline this year's festival. Past performers: Jim & Jesse, Cox Family, Ralph Stanley,

---

A = wheelchair accessible   I = interpreter for hearing impaired   F = food   FF = fast food   EF = ethnic food
VF = vegetarian food   RF = regional food   R = restaurants nearby   P = pets welcome   CC = credit cards

Wilma Lee Cooper, New Coon Creek Girls. Performances held both indoors and outdoors. A covered area is available for the audience outdoors. Workshops, children's activities and crafts. Hours: 11 a.m.-5 p.m. both days. Tickets: adults $9 per day. Age 60+ $8 per day. Children (4-12) $7. A, F, R, MR, CO, RVN, HN, M

Contact: Terry M. Lease, Downstate Illinois Bluegrass Assoc., P.O. Box 456, Jacksonville, IL 62651 • Phone: 217-243-3159

Winter Indoor Bluegrass Festival
January 26-28
Holiday Inn, Qunicy, IL

Since 1988. Annual attendance is 2,000. Lots of jamming at this fun family event. This year's headliners: Jim & Jesse, Sally Mountain Show, Randall Hylton, and 4 other bands. Past performers: Lost & Found, Cox Family. Children's activities and crafts area. All performances held indoors. Hours: Friday 7:30 p.m. through Sunday 3:00 p.m. Tickets: $15 for the weekend. Per show: $6 and up. Children admitted at half price. A, F (full service on site), MR, S, M (festival held at motel).

Contact: Terry M. Lease, Downstate Illinois Bluegrass Assoc., P.O. Box 456, Jacksonville, IL 62651 • Phone: 217-243-3159

Indiana

4th Annual Lawrenceburg Bluegrass Festival
August 9-10
Lawrenceburg Fairgrounds, Lawrenceburg, IN

Since 1993. Annual attendance is 1,000. Bill Monroe helped to launch this festival and "put it on the bluegrass map." Past performers include Bill Monroe and The Blue Grass Boys. This year's headliners are the Sand Mountain Boys and The Larry Stephenson Band. All performances held outdoors. Hours: Friday 6 p.m.-11 p.m., Saturday 2 p.m.-11 p.m. Call for ticket prices. Advance ticket sales available. A, FF, R, MR, RVO, HO, M

Contact: Bob Mills, 377 Tower Road, Lawrenceburg, IN 47025 • Phone: 812-537-4531

Bean Blossom Bluegrass Festival
June 20-23, September 13-15
Bill & James Monroe Park, Bean Blossom, IN

Since 1966. This is the oldest continually running bluegrass festival in the United States, held at a park owned by Bill Monroe. Bill Monroe is a featured guest each year. Showcases mainly nationally known acts. Past performances by Ralph Stanley.

MR = modern restrooms   RR = rustic restrooms   CO = camping on-site   CN = camping nearby   S = hot showers
RVO = RVs on-site   RVN = RVs nearby   HO = hookups on-site   HN = hookups nearby   M = motels nearby

All performances held outdoors. Crafts area. Hours: noon to midnight. Ticket prices vary from year to year; call for specific information. A, FF, RF, R, P (on leash), RR, CO, CN, RVO, RVN, HO, HN, M

Contact: Jim Bessire, Bean Blossom Bluegrass Festival, 3819 Dickerson Road, Nashville, TN 37207 • Phone: 615-868-3333 • Fax: 615-868-7347

OFFICIAL INDIANA PICKIN' & FIDDLIN' CONTEST
June 7-8
Prides Creek Park, Petersburg, IN

Since 1983. Annual attendance is 2,000. This is the official Indiana state pickin' and fiddlin' contest and is sanctioned by the National Old Time Fiddlers Association. This year's headliner: The Young Acoustic Allstars. Past performers: Lonzo & Oscar, Bill Stewart, The Patoka Valley Boys. Children's activities and crafts area. All performances held outdoors. Events begin Friday at 7 p.m. and Saturday at 10 a.m. Admission is $2 for Friday and $5 for Saturday. A, FF, R, P, MR, RR, CN, S, RVO, RVN, HO, HN, M

Contact: Tony Rothrock, 4139 S. 300, E. Winslow, IN 47598 • Phone: 812-789-2518

STONEY RUN BLUEGRASS FESTIVAL
August 3-4
Stoney Run County Park, Leroy, IN

Since 1978. Annual attendance is 2,500. Features traditional bluegrass and gospel music. Held in Stoney Run Park, one of the most beautiful parks in Indiana, this festival has a relaxed, family atmosphere. Surrounded by miles of hiking trails and an abundance of wildlife, the town is home to the Lake County Vietnam Veterans Memorial. A high-quality lineup of artists is expected for this year's event. Past performers: The Cox Family, New Tradition, The Rarely Herd, The Stevens Family, Petticoat Junction, The Sand Mountain Boys. Children's activities. Impromptu audience dancing. All performances held outdoors. Hours: open mic 9-11 a.m., music 11 a.m.-7:30 p.m. Tickets: $8 advance, $10 at the gate. Children (12 and under) admitted free with paid adult. Weekend camping passes $18 in advance, $22 at the gate. A, I (upon request), FF, R, P (not in viewing area), CC, RR, CO, RVO, M

Contact: Jim Cadwell, Stoney Run Bluegrass Festival, 2293 N. Main Street, Crown Point, IN 46307 • Phone: 219-769-7275 or 219-663-8170 • Fax: 219-663-0769

THE INDY CLASSIC BLUEGRASS FESTIVAL
March 8-10
Ramada Hotel – Airport, I-465 exit 11-B, Indianapolis, IN

Since 1995. Expected attendance is 2,500. Held at a convenient location in a great hotel, this festival features top-name performers. This year's headliners: Cox Family, Ralph Stanley, Warrior River Boys, Charlie Sizemore, New Vintage, and 5 other bands. Workshops, children's activities, crafts area. All performances held indoors. Hours:

A = wheelchair accessible   I = interpreter for hearing impaired   F = food   FF = fast food   EF = ethnic food
VF = vegetarian food   RF = regional food   R = restaurants nearby   P = pets welcome   CC = credit cards

Friday 7:30 p.m. through Sunday 3:30 p.m. Weekend pass is $25; per show is $10 and up. Children admitted half price. Advance ticket sales available. A, F (full service on site), R, MR, S, M (festival held at hotel)

Contact: Terry M. Lease, Downstate Illinois Bluegrass Assoc., P.O. Box 456, Jacksonville, IL 62651 • Phone: 217-243-3159

Iowa

10TH ANNUAL BLUEGRASS MUSIC WEEKEND
March 29-31
Ramada Inn, Burlington, IA

Since 1987. Annual attendance is 1,500. Features top name bands. Workshops, children's activities, crafts area. All performances held indoors. Hours: 9-12. Tickets: $16. A, F (restaurant on site), R, MR, RVN, M

Contact: Delbert Spray, Annual Bluegrass Music Weekend/Burlington, RR 1, Box 71, Kahoka, MO 63445 • Phone: 314-853-4344

10TH ANNUAL FALL BLUEGRASS FESTIVAL
November 1-3
Iowan Motor Lodge, Ft. Madison, IA

Since 1986. Annual attendance is 1,500. Features top name bluegrass bands. Workshops, children's activities, crafts area. All performances held indoors. Hours: 12-12. Tickets: $18. A, F, R, RVN, M

Contact: Delbert Spray, Annual Fall Bluegrass Festival, RR 1, Box 71, Kahoka, MO 63445 • Phone: 314-853-4344

2ND ANNUAL MEMORIAL DAY BLUEGRASS FESTIVAL
May 24-26
Des Moines County Fairgrounds, Burlington, IA

Since 1995. Annual attendance is 1,000. Features top name bluegrass bands. Musical competitions, workshops, children's activities, crafts area. All performances held outdoors. A covered area is available for the audience. Hours: 9-12. Tickets: $20. A, FF, R, P, MR, S, RVO, RVN, HO, HN, M

Contact: Delbert Spray, Memorial Day Bluegrass Festival, RR 1, Box 70, Kahoka, MO 63445 • Contact: 314-853-4344

MR = modern restrooms   RR = rustic restrooms   CO = camping on-site   CN = camping nearby   S = hot showers
RVO = RVs on-site   RVN = RVs nearby   HO = hookups on-site   HN = hookups nearby   M = motels nearby

BACKBONE BLUEGRASS FESTIVAL
July 26-28
off Hwy. 3 on W. 69, Forrestville Rd., 2 mi. south of Strawberry Point, IA

Since 1981. Annual attendance is 4,000 to 5,000. This festival features bluegrass, country and gospel music performed on private grounds with plenty of shade trees. The organizers strive to make attendees comfortable and happy, and many people take early vacations and spend a week at the campgrounds. It's been described as a "big family get together." This year's headliners include Bluestem, Toganoxie Kansas, Bob Lewis Family Band, Chapman Family, Colorado, and many others. Past performers: Mike Snyder, Alison Krauss & Union Station, The Cox Family. Workshops, children's activities, and crafts area. Performances are Friday at 7 p.m., Saturday 1 p.m. and 7 p.m., and Sunday 9:30 a.m. and 12:30 p.m. Advance tickets (before July 1st): Friday $6, Saturday all day $8, Sunday $4, weekend pass $17. At the gate: Friday $7, Saturday $9, Sunday $5, weekend pass $19. A, F (restaurant on grounds), R, P, RR, CO, S, RVO, RVN, HO, HN, M (small town; reservations needed by 3/96)

Contact: Doris Baker, Backbone Bluegrass Festival, P.O. Box 438, Strawberry Point, IA 52076 • Phone: 319-933-4331

THE HAWKEYE SPECIAL BLUEGRASS FESTIVAL
January 13-15
Jumer Castle Lodge Hotel, I-74 Exit, Spruce Hills Road, Bettendorf, IA

Since 1995. Expected attendance is 2,500. A great lineup of bands perform in a warm and comfortable hotel environment. No alcohol or smoking permitted in the concert room. This year's headliners: Lost & Found, Rarely Herd, Stevens Family, Dry Branch Fire Squad, and more. Past performers: Cox Family, John Hartford. Crafts area. Hours: Friday 7:30 p.m. through Sunday 4 p.m. Tickets are $20 for a weekend pass. Individual day passes start at $10. Children are admitted at half price. A, F (full service on site), R, MR, S, M (festival held at hotel)

Contact: Terry M. Lease, Downstate Illinois Bluegrass Assoc., P.O. Box 456, Jacksonville, IL 62651 • Phone: 217-243-3159

Kansas

3RD ANNUAL PARK CITY BLUEGRASS FESTIVAL
May 3-4
Kansas Coliseum, Park City, KS

Since 1994. Annual attendance is 500 to 800. Features a weekend of bluegrass music at a great price. This year's headliners: IIIrd Tyme Out, The Chapman Family. Past performers: California, Rarely Herd, The Stevens Family, Red Oak. Children's activities, crafts area, and clogging. All performances held indoors. Hours: noon-

---

A = wheelchair accessible   I = interpreter for hearing impaired   F = food   FF = fast food   EF = ethnic food
VF = vegetarian food   RF = regional food   R = restaurants nearby   P = pets welcome   CC = credit cards

11 p.m. both days. Price: $3 button for the complete festival. A, FF, R, P, MR, S, RVO, RVN, HO, HN, M

Contact: Jim Bullard, Annual Park City Bluegrass Festival, 7 Rolling Hills, Wichita, KS 67212 • Phone: 316-722-6241

25TH ANNUAL WALNUT VALLEY FESTIVAL & INTERNATIONAL FLATPICKING CHAMPIONSHIPS
September 19-22
Cowley County Fairgrounds, Winfield, KS

Since 1972. Annual attendance is 12,000. Designed as family entertainment, all kinds of acoustic music combine to form the heart of this festival at the Cowley County Fairgrounds, surrounded by campgrounds amid the natural beauty of the Walnut River. National and international contests, workshops, children's events, a large arts & crafts fair, 20 luthiers, 30 entertainer acts, and over 150 hours of concerts and all-night campground picking make this the International Convention for Acoustic String Musicians (also known as "Pickers Paradise"). Past headliners: Lester Flatt, Doc & Merle Watson, Merle Travis, Alison Krauss, Mark O'Connor, Jimmy Driftwood, Norman Blake, Tom Chapin, John McCutcheon, Mike Seeger, Bryan Bowers, Tony Rice, New Grass Revival, Tom Paxton. Children's activities and Irish dancing. Performances held both indoors and outdoors, with a covered area outdoors for the audience. Hours: 9 a.m.-midnight. Tickets: $48 to $60 for a 4-day pass. Advance ticket sales available. A (most areas), I, FF, EF, VF, RF, R, MR, RR, CO, CN, S, RVO, RVN, HO, HN, M

Contact: Bob L. Redford, P.O. Box 245, Winfield, KS 67156 • Phone: 316-221-3250 • Fax: 316-221-3109

SAWLOG 'N' STRINGS BLUEGRASS & FOLK FESTIVAL
August 17-18
Warner Grove, Dodge City, KS

Since 1990. Annual attendance is 860. Warner Grove was planted in the 1880s. It is a fairytale-like, densely shaded, hardwood atmosphere of seclusion with a feeling of old-fashioned living including free wagon rides behind Percheron draft horses. Bluegrass and folk music are featured. Past performers: Echo Creek, Chapman Family, Hot Pursuit, Bluegrass Country, New Oldtimers, The Raleys, and Prairie Wind. Workshops, children's activities, crafts and clog dancing. All performances are held outdoors under huge shade tress. Hours are 9 a.m. August 17 through 5 p.m. August 18. Ticket prices: $8 ($7 in advance), children (under 16) free. Senior citizens buses are $1 per person. A, FF, EF, P, RR, CO, CN, RVO, RVN, HN, M

Contact: Ron or Diane Cole, Rt. 1, Box 28, Jetmore, KS 67854-9708 • Phone: 316-357-6534 or 316-385-2456

MR = modern restrooms   RR = rustic restrooms   CO = camping on-site   CN = camping nearby   S = hot showers
RVO = RVs on-site   RVN = RVs nearby   HO = hookups on-site   HN = hookups nearby   M = motels nearby

Kentucky

BLUEGRASS IN THE PARK
August 1-3
Central Park, Henderson, KY

Since 1985. Annual attendance is 6,000 to 8,000. This festival showcases traditional and progressive bluegrass from local, regional, and national bands and performers, as well as gospel music. It is a free festival, underwritten by the area's local Arts Alliance and Rotary Club. The only admission fee is on the first night of the festival which is held at the Fine Arts Center. The festival is held in the oldest city park west of the Appalachians. Past performers: Bill Monroe & The Blue Grass Boys, IIIrd Tyme Out, Lonesome River Band, Dry Branch Fire Squad, The Doug Dillard Band, Continental Divide, The Bluegrass Cardinals, and many more. Performances are both indoors and outdoors. Hours vary. A, RF, R, MR, RR, CN, RVN, HN, M

Contact: Ken Christopher, Bluegrass in the Park, 115 Clay Street, Henderson, KY 42420 • Phone: 502-831-1200 • Fax: 502-831-1206

CUMBERLAND MOUNTAIN FALL FESTIVAL
October 11-13
City Parking Lot, N. 20th Street, Middlesboro, KY

Since 1984. Annual attendance is 30,000 to 40,000. Middlesboro is a very unique community of about 12,000 nestled in the Appalachian Mountains. It is located at the Cumberland Gap where pioneers from Pennsylvania, Virginia and the Carolinas took the Wilderness Trail through that natural pass, in the footsteps of Daniel Boone. Today that trail is the Cumberland Gap National Historical Park. Its 20,000 acres extend into Tennessee, Virginia and Kentucky, making it the largest historic park in the country. That, coupled with Pine Mountain State Resort Park on its north side, make Middlesboro a popular tourist area. The festival focuses on country, bluegrass and gospel music. Each year the festival hosts the official Kentucky "Governor's Cup Banjo Championship." It also features a wide range of musical artists, a carnival, juried crafts from nearly a dozen states along with artist demonstrations, children's activities, antique and classic car show, pet show, petting zoo and lots more. Dancing includes line dance, street dance and clogging. Past performers include Alison Krauss, Clinton Gregory, Daron Norwood, Mid South, Matthews-Wright & King. All events are held outdoors. Hours are 9 a.m.-9 p.m. October 11 & 12, and noon-6 p.m. October 13. Admission is $1 for the 3-day period. A (on parking lot), FF, EF, RF, R, P, RR, RVO, RVN, M

Contact: Alice Harris, Cumberland Mountain Fall Festival, P.O. Box 788, Middlesboro, KY 40965 • Phone: 606-248-1075 or 1-800-988-1075 • Fax: 606-248-8851

A = wheelchair accessible   I = interpreter for hearing impaired   F = food   FF = fast food   EF = ethnic food
VF = vegetarian food   RF = regional food   R = restaurants nearby   P = pets welcome   CC = credit cards

FIDDLERS' FESTIVAL
November 1-3
Renfro Valley Entertainment Center, Renfro Valley, KY

Since 1983. This is an "old time" gathering — sharing music, memories, fellowship, and the appreciation of the fiddle. Features bluegrass, country and gospel music, with over 50 fiddle players on stage at one time! Past performers: Jim Gaskin, Bobby Slone, The Eversole Brothers. Children's activities and crafts area. All performances held indoors. Hours: Friday 7 p.m. to ??, Saturday 10 a.m.-noon and 1 p.m.-4 p.m., Sunday 1 p.m. to ??. No charge to fiddle players and musicians performing. Tickets are $6 per show. Weekend pass and advance ticket sales available. A, FF, RF, R, P (RV park and outside village area only), CC, MR, CN, S, RVO, RVN, HO, HN, M

Contact: Cindy Roberts, Fiddlers' Festival, Renfro Valley Entertainment Center, Renfro Valley, KY 40473 • Phone: 800-765-7464 or 606-256-2638 • Fax: 606-256-2679

IBMA BLUEGRASS FAN FEST '96
September 20-22
English Park, Owensboro, KY

Since 1986. Annual attendance is 8,500. IBMA Bluegrass Fan Fest is the weekend culmination of the annual IBMA World of Bluegrass trade show, convention and awards show. An international homecoming of sorts, the week is also an opportunity for individuals involved in various aspects of the bluegrass music industry to come together and learn from each other, to recognize special achievements for the year, and to advance their careers. Half of the proceeds from Fan Fest, the outdoor bluegrass festival at nearby English Park in Owensboro, Kentucky, go to benefit the Bluegrass Trust Fund, which provides financial assistance for bluegrass artists in times of dire need and emergencies. Fan Fest features the very top-of-the-line bluegrass acts, artist instrumental workshops by the "masters," children's activities, industry-related booths, and food vendors. Past performers include: Alison Krauss, Laurie Lewis, Doc Watson, Jim & Jesse, The Cox Family, Nashville Bluegrass Band, Third Tyme Out, Lonesome Standard Time, Claire Lynch, Doyle Lawson, Lynn Morrison, Tony Rice, Jerry Douglas, Bela Fleck, Sam Bush, The Whites, Del McCoury Band, The Sidemen, Tim O'Brien. All performances are held outdoors. Hours are Friday 4-11 p.m., Saturday noon-11 p.m., Sunday 11 a.m.-5 p.m. Call for ticket prices. Advance sales available. A, FF, RF, R, CC, RR, CO, CN, RVO, RVN, HN, M

Contact: Dan Hays, 207 E. Second Street, Owensboro, KY 42301 • Phone: 502-684-9025 • Fax: 502-686-7863

JACKSONIAN DAYS
April 20
Public Square, Scottsville, KY

The festival features Bluegrass Jamboree competitions, an arts and crafts show and sale, 5K run, a fun run and health walk, children's games, food court, antique car

---

MR = modern restrooms   RR = rustic restrooms   CO = camping on-site   CN = camping nearby   S = hot showers
RVO = RVs on-site   RVN = RVs nearby   HO = hookups on-site   HN = hookups nearby   M = motels nearby

show, quilt show. All events are outdoors. Hours are 8-6 daily. Admission is free. A, FF, EF, RF, R, P, RR, RVN, HN, M

Contact: Sue Shaver, Jacksonian Days, P.O. Box 416, Scottsville, KY 42164 • Phone: 502-237-4782

New Coon Creek Girls Bluegrass Festival
August 30-September 1
Renfro Valley Entertainment Center, Renfro Valley, KY

Since 1992. Annual attendance is 7,000 to 10,000. The Coon Creek Girls invite some of their bluegrass friends to the festival grounds for three days of bluegrass picking and singing. This year's headliners: The Reno Brothers, Doyle Lawson & Quicksilver, Glen Duncan. Past performers: Southern Blend, The Osborne Brothers, Southern Harvest. All performances held outdoors. A covered area is available for the audience. Crafts area. Hours: Friday 3:30 p.m.-10:30 p.m., Saturday 12:30-10:30 p.m., Sunday 12:30-8:30 p.m. Advance tickets 1-2-3: $14, $22, $29. At the gate 1-2-3: $14, $24, $31. A, FF, EF, RF, R, P (camping area only), CC, MR, RR, CO, CN, S, RVO, RVN, HO, HN, M

Contact: Cindy Roberts, New Coon Creek Girls BG Festival, Renfro Valley Entertainment Center, Renfro Valley, KY 40473 • Phone: 800-765-7464 or 606-256-2638 • Fax: 606-256-2679

Official Kentucky State Championship Old-Time Fiddlers Contest Inc.
July 19-20
Rough River Dam State Resort Park, Leitchfield, KY

Since 1974. Annual attendance is 2,000 to 3,000. This is a nonprofit event, sponsored by the Rotary Club for local projects. It is completely locally funded and self-supported. Features old-time fiddle and bluegrass music, competitions for children and adults, crafts and jig dancing. All performances held outdoors. Hours are Friday, 7 p.m.-11 p.m., and Saturday 10 a.m.-11 p.m. Tickets prices: Friday $5, Saturday $8. Two-day tickets $12. A, FF, RF, R, P (on leash), RR, CO, S, RVO, HO, CN, RVN, HN, M

Contact: Brent L. Miller, Leitchfield Rotary Club, P.O. Box 4042, Leitchfield, KY 42755 • Phone: 502-259-3578

Old Joe Clark Bluegrass Festival
July 5-7
Renfro Valley Entertainment Center, Renfro Valley, KY

Since 1970's. Annual attendance is 10,000 to 12,000. A wide variety of great bluegrass pickers and singers gather in the festival grounds for music filled days and nights. This year's headliners: Osborne Brothers, Lewis Family, Stevens Family, New Coon Creek Girls, and, of course, Old Joe and Terry Clark. Past performers include Rarely

A = wheelchair accessible   I = interpreter for hearing impaired   F = food   FF = fast food   EF = ethnic food
VF = vegetarian food   RF = regional food   R = restaurants nearby   P = pets welcome   CC = credit cards

Herd, Lonesome River Band, Traditional Grass, Raymond Fairchild. All performances held outdoors. A covered area is available for the audience. Crafts area. Hours: Friday 3:30 p.m.-11:30 p.m., Saturday noon-11:30 p.m., Sunday noon-9 p.m. Advance tickets 1-2-3: $14, $22, $29. At the gate 1-2-3: $14, $24, $31. A, FF, EF, RF, R, P (camping area only), CC, MR, RR, CO, CN, S, RVO, RVN, HO, HN, M

Contact: Cindy Roberts, Old Joe Clark Bluegrass Festival, Renfro Valley Entertainment Center, Renfro Valley, KY 40473 • Phone: 606-256-2638 • Fax: 606-256-2679

POPPY MOUNTAIN BLUEGRASS FEST
September 17-21
Poppy Mountain, Morehead, KY

Since 1993. Annual attendance is 5,000 to 10,000. In addition to fabulous bluegrass music, this festival offers old-fashioned buggy rides, horse riding, mule-pulled hay rides, free firewood for everyone, 1,000 acres to roam, fishing lakes all at walking distance, and the director of the festival on site. This year's headliners: Larry Sparks, Ralph Stanley, Osborne Brothers, and about 22 bands in all. Past performers: Alison Krauss & Union Station, Ralph Stanley, Osborne Brothers, Larry Sparks, Rarely Herd, and many, many more. Musical competitions, workshops, children's activities, crafts and traditional dancing. Most performances outdoors. Hours are noon to midnight. Tickets for the entire event are $25 in advance, $30 at the gate. A, FF, EF, VF, RF, R, P (on leash), MR, RR, CO, CN, S, RVO, RVN, HO, HN, M

Contact: Marty Stevens, U.S. 60 East, Box 8030, Morehead, KY 40351 • Phone: 606-784-2277 or 606-784-1810 • Fax: 606-784-5439

ROSINE 23RD ANNUAL BLUEGRASS HOMECOMING
June 28-29
Ohio County Park, Hartford, KY

Since 1973. Annual attendance is 500 to 5,000. The home of Bill Monroe and bluegrass music. Past performers: Bill Monroe, Jimmy Martin, Gillis Brothers, Coon Creek Girls, Jim & Jesse, Bill Herald, IIIrd Tyme Out. Hours: Friday 5 p.m.-midnight, Saturday 11 a.m.-11:45 p.m. All performances held outdoors. Call for ticket information. A, FF, R, MR, CO, S, RVO, HO, M

Contact: Stoy L. Geary, P.O. Box 336, Rosine, KY 42370 • Phone: 502-274-4700

SPRING HOLLER BLUEGRASS FESTIVAL
August 9-11
Harold Austin's Old Homeplace, Casey Co., Dunnville, KY

Since 1990. Annual attendance is 1,000 to 2,500. This is Kentucky hospitality at its best with plenty of Southern-style bluegrass music, real friendly people and good Southern cooking. Everyone is welcome. ("You all come!") This year's headliner: Harold Austin & The First National Bluegrass. Crafts area and traditional dancing.

MR = modern restrooms   RR = rustic restrooms   CO = camping on-site   CN = camping nearby   S = hot showers
RVO = RVs on-site   RVN = RVs nearby   HO = hookups on-site   HN = hookups nearby   M = motels nearby

All performances held outdoors. A covered area is available for the audience. Hours: 1 p.m.-midnight. Call for ticket prices. FF, EF, VF, R, RR, CO, CN, M

Contact: Harold Austin, Spring Holler Bluegrass Festival, Rt. 1, Box 244, Dunnville, KY 42528 • Phone: 606-787-5152

Maine

19TH ANNUAL THOMAS POINT BEACH BLUEGRASS FESTIVAL
August 30-September 1 (call to confirm)
Thomas Pt. Beach, Brunswick, ME

Since 1979. This festival is recognized for its World Class Bluegrass Entertainers, professional services, scenic coastal site and friendly atmosphere. Features music all week long with top national acts – Bill Monroe, Ralph Stanley, Alison Krauss, Johnson Mountain Boys, Jim & Jesse, Bill Harrell, Mac Wiseman, J.D. Crowe, Lewis Family, Raymond Fairchild, Cox Family, Larry Stephenson Band, Canadian Grass Unit, Emerson & Taylor, and many, many more! Over 18 bands. Field pickin', 24-hour food, security, and medical available. Sunday morning service on the beach. Free camping. Excellent stage show. New England's #1 family festival! All performances held outdoors. A covered area is available for the audience. Musical competitions, children's activities and crafts area. Hours: 9-9 daily. Call for ticket prices. Children under 12 admitted free. Advance ticket sales available. A, F, R, MR, RR, CO, CN, S, RVO, RVN, HO, M

Contact: Patricia M. Crooker, Thomas Point Beach Bluegrass Festival, 29 Meadow Road, Brunswick, ME 04011 • Phone: 207-725-6009

24TH ANNUAL EAST BENTON FIDDLERS CONVENTION
July 29
Littlefield Farm, East Benton, ME

Since 1972. Annual attendance is 2,000+. Held in a natural amphitheatre surrounded by pine trees, this festival is a like an old-fashioned family reunion. Good food, good country people, and the love of bluegrass and folk music. Includes 3 fiddle contests (juniors, adults and seniors). Crafts area and impromptu dancing (folk and traditional) in the field. Past performers: Freddie Carpenter, Yodeling Slim Clark, Blistered Fingers, and many other bluegrass bands. All performances held outdoors. Hours are 12 to dusk. Tickets: $7 for adults, children (under 14) admitted free. Advance ticket sales available. A, FF, VF, R, RR, CN, RVN, HN, M

Contact: Shirley Littlefield, East Benton Fiddle Convention, Box 215, Clinton, ME 04927 • Phone: 207-453-2017

A = wheelchair accessible   I = interpreter for hearing impaired   F = food   FF = fast food   EF = ethnic food
VF = vegetarian food   RF = regional food   R = restaurants nearby   P = pets welcome   CC = credit cards

BLISTERED FINGERS 6TH ANNUAL FAMILY BLUEGRASS MUSIC FESTIVAL
June 13-16
Silver Spur Riding Club, Exit #32, Sidney, ME

Since 1991. Annual attendance is 1,000. Exceptionally friendly, family atmosphere in a lovely, easy-to-find location. Kids events and a great lineup of performers. This year's headliners: Rhonda Vincent, Lewis Family, Freddy Clark Family, Lynn Morris, Blistered Fingers, and more. Past performers: Jimmy Martin, Kenny Baker, Josh Graves, Sally Mountain Show, Lewis Family, Stevens Family, Cox Family, Bob Lewis Family, Warrior River Boys, Blistered Fingers. Crafts area and traditional dancing. All performances except children's acts are held outdoors. There is a covered area available for the audience. Hours: Thursday 6 p.m.-10 p.m., Friday 4 p.m.-10 p.m., Saturday 10 a.m.-10 p.m., Sunday 10 a.m.-6 p.m. Call for ticket prices. Advance ticket sales available. A, FF, EF, VF, RF, R, P, RR, RVO, RVN, HO, HN, M

Contact: Sandy Cormier, RFD 1, Box 7560, Waterville, ME 04901 • Phone: 207-873-6539

HEBRON PINES BLUEGRASS FESTIVAL
May 23-26
Hebron Pines Campground, Hebron, ME

Since 1990. Annual attendance 2,000. This festival is small enough to be friendly and large enough to be modern, drawing top notch bluegrass entertainment. This year's headliners: Bill Harrell & The Virginians. Past performers: Red & Murphy & Their Excellent Children. Musical competitions and workshops. All performances held outdoors. A covered area is available for the audience. Hours: Friday 6-9:45 p.m., Saturday 10 a.m.-9:20 p.m., Sunday 10 a.m.-9:20 p.m. Tickets: 3-day advance $27, at gate $30. Friday $8. After 5 p.m. Friday and Saturday $8. Seniors receive 10% discount. A, FF, RF, R, P, CC, MR, CO, CN, S, RVO, RVN, HO, HN, M

Contact: Gary Kyllonen, Hebron Pines Bluegrass Festival, R.R. 1, Box 1955, Hebron, ME 04238 • Phone: 207-966-2179

OXFORD COUNTY BLUEGRASS FESTIVAL
August 16-18
Rose-Beck Farm, S. Paris, ME

Since 1986. Annual attendance is 1,500 to 2,000. This festival is held in the beautiful Oxford Hills area of western Maine. The setting is in the lush green fields of Rose-Beck Farm with a farm pond nearby and an old county road through the woods for long walks. This year's headliners: Traver Hollow, White Mountain Bluegrass, Bob Paisely. Past performers: Carl Story, Mac Wiseman, Wilma Lee Cooper, Hylo Brown, White Mountain, Traver Hollow, Southern Rail. Musical competitions with the open stage winner hired for the following year. Crafts area. All performances held outdoors. A covered area is available for the audience outdoors. Hours: Friday 6 p.m. through

---

MR = modern restrooms   RR = rustic restrooms   CO = camping on-site   CN = camping nearby   S = hot showers
RVO = RVs on-site   RVN = RVs nearby   HO = hookups on-site   HN = hookups nearby   M = motels nearby

Sunday 5 p.m. Tickets: 3-day advance $25, 3-day at the gate $28, Friday $8, Saturday $16 (after 5 p.m. $8), Sunday $8. A, FF, EF, R, P, RR, CO, CN, RVO, RVN, HN, M

Contact: Sidney or Nancy Record, Oxford County Bluegrass Festival, 486 E. Oxford Road, S. Paris, ME 04281 • Phone: 207-743-2905

Maryland

13TH ANNUAL ARCADIA BLUEGRASS FESTIVAL
September 26-29
Arcadia Firemen's Grounds, Upperco, MD

Since 1984. Annual attendance is 1,000± per day. This is a family-oriented festival sponsored by the membership of the Arcadia Volunteer Fire Company. Friendly atmosphere, plenty of good ol' parking lot picking. Rowdy behavior is not allowed. Security on duty. Past performers: Mac Wiseman, Osborne Brothers, Lewis Family, Larry Sparks, Jim & Jesse, Boys From Indiana, Larry Stephenson, Ralph Stanley. All performances held outdoors. A covered area is available for the audience. Crafts area. Hours: Thursday 7-11 p.m., Friday 4 p.m.-midnight, Saturday 11 a.m.-midnight, Sunday 10 a.m.-6 p.m. Advance three-day pass includes Thursday admission at no charge. Per day tickets also available. Call for prices. A, FF, RF, R, P (on leash, but not in concession or concert areas), RR, CO, S, RVO, HO, M

Contact: William Hale, Jr., Chairman, Arcadia Bluegrass Festival, 15723 Dover Road, Upperco, MD 21155 • Phone: 410-374-2895

19TH ANNUAL GRANTSVILLE DAYS
June 28-30
Grantsville Park, Grantsville, MD

Since 1977. Annual attendance is 14,000. Features bluegrass and country rock music along with a talent exhibition. Local homecoming event. No commercial food vendors. Tractor and horse pulling contest. Games for all. Western line dancing. All events held outdoors. Hours: Friday 7:15 p.m.-11 p.m., Saturday noon-11 p.m., Sunday noon-5 p.m. Admission is free. A, F, R, P, MR, CN, RVN, HN, M

Contact: Garrett Co. Promotion Council, P.O. Box 450, Grantsville, MD 21536 • Phone: 301-334-1948

29TH ANNUAL AUTUMN GLORY FESTIVAL
October 10-13
Oakland (and surrounding area), MD

Since 1968. Annual attendance is 50,000 to 60,000. This 4-day festival is held annually at the peak of the fall foliage season in mid-October and attracts visitors from all over the country. It features bluegrass, fiddle, banjo, and gospel music, as well as

---

A = wheelchair accessible   I = interpreter for hearing impaired   F = food   FF = fast food   EF = ethnic food
VF = vegetarian food   RF = regional food   R = restaurants nearby   P = pets welcome   CC = credit cards

activities for the whole family. Additional festivities include 2 big parades and firemen's events, arts, crafts, antiques, and more. It was named one of the top 100 events in N. America by the American Business Association in 1995. Past performers: Waylon Jennings, Ricky Skaggs, The New Coon Creek Girls. Performances held both indoors and outdoors. Musical competitions, crafts area, and square dancing. A variety of food vendors. Hours vary. Some activities require admission; many are free. Advance ticket sales are available for some events. A, F, R, CC, MR, RR, CN, RVN, HN, M

Contact: Diane Wolfe, 200 South Third Street, Oakland, MD 21550 • Phone: 301-334-1948 • Fax: 301-334-1919

4TH ANNUAL BERLIN FIDDLER'S CONVENTION
September 28
Atlantic Hotel, Berlin, MD

Since 1993. Annual attendance is 5,000. This festival features bluegrass and country music performed in the historic Atlantic Hotel which is over 100 years old. Located 6 miles from the Atlantic Ocean and Ocean City, Maryland, it offers good, clean family fun and entertainment. Musical competitions, children's activities and crafts. Hours: 11 a.m.-4 p.m. Admission is free. A, F, R, P, MR, RVN, HN, M

Contact: Frank W. Nanna, 6428 South Point Road, Berlin, MD 21811 • Phone: 410-641-4151 • Fax: same (call first)

COMER BROTHERS BLUEGRASS FESTIVAL
July 4-7
1640 Poole Road, Darlington, MD

Since 1992. Annual attendance is 1,500 to 2,000. Offers the best home-cooked food of any festival (according to the organizers). Run by a family that loves bluegrass music, musicians and all bluegrass people. Good family festival with a great lineup year after year. Past performers: Alison Krauss & Union Station, Jim & Jesse & The Virginia Boys, Jimmy Martin, The Lewis Family, IIIrd Tyme Out, Traditional Grass, Lost & Found, Lonesome River Band, Bass Mountain Boys, Gillis Brothers, Boys From Indiana, Bluegrass Cardinals. Children's activities and crafts area. All performances held outdoors. A covered area is available for the audience. Hours: 4th 3 p.m.-midnight, 5th 1 p.m.-midnight, 6th 10 a.m.-midnight, 7th 10 a.m.-5 p.m. Tickets: Thursday $7, Friday $18, Saturday $25, Sunday $15. Weekend pass $45 advance, $50 at the gate. Cutoff for advance sales is June 15th. A, FF, RF, R, RR, CO, CN, RVO, RVN, HN, M

Contact: Susie Comer, Comer Brothers Bluegrass Festival, 2100 Slade Lane, Forest Hill, MD 21050 • Phone: 410-879-6699 or 800-332-5715 • Fax: 410-638-0289

FRIENDSVILLE FIDDLER'S & BANJO CONTEST
July 20
Town Park, Friendsville, MD

Since 1964. Annual attendance is 300. The small historic town of Friendsville showcases American fiddle and banjo music in 3 age categories: Junior Division (16 and under), Middle Division (17 through 59), and Senior Division (60 and over) encompassing bluegrass and traditional American country music. All events held outdoors. A covered area is available for the audience. Traditional dancing. Contest begins at 7 p.m. Tickets: $5 adult, $2 children (16 and under). A, F, R, MR, CN, M

Contact: Mary or Albert Walcek, 133 Claude Fike Road, Accident, MD 21520 • Phone: 301-746-8194

KING OYSTER'S BLUEGRASS REVUE
October 19
St. Mary's County Fairgrounds, Leonardtown, MD

Since 1994. Annual attendance is 15,000 to 20,000. Features bluegrass music and hosts the National Oyster Shucking Contest. This year's headliner: Eastern Tradition. Past performers: Lynn Morris Band, Eastern Tradition, Stevens Family, Gary Brewer & Kentucky Ramblers. Children's activities and crafts area. Aerobic dancing. Performances held both indoors and outdoors. A covered area is available for the audience outdoors. Hours: 4:30 p.m. until ??. Tickets: $3. A, RF, R, RR, CN, RVN, HN, M

Contact: Jay Armsworthy, King Oyster's Bluegrass Revue, 6648 Three Notch Road, California, MD 20619 • Phone: 301-862-2925

LITTLE MARGARET'S BLUEGRASS & OLD-TIME COUNTRY MUSIC FESTIVAL
August 8-11
Goddard Farm, St. Mary's County, Leonardtown, MD

Since 1989. Annual attendance is 500 to 800. This is a family-style festival which attracts a specific group of people. The location is lovely with flowers and green grass on the side of a hill. Bluegrass and old-time country music are featured. Past performers: Mac Wiseman, The Osborne Brothers, Sand Mountain Boys, Country Current Bluegrass Ensemble (US Navy Band), Dean Sapp & Hartford Express. Children's activities, crafts area, dancing (clogging and squares), and home-cooked meals. All performances are held outdoors. A covered area is available for the audience. Hours: Thursday 6-12, Friday 4-12, Saturday 10-12, and Sunday 10-5. Tickets: $30 for the weekend, Friday $12, Saturday $15, Sunday $12. Advance discount (before July 1) is $27 for the weekend. A, FF, RF, R, P (kept at campsite; not in concert area), RR, RVO, RVN, HO, HN, M

Contact: Joseph H. Goddard, Rt. 1, Box 85A, Leonardtown, MD 20650 • Phone: 301-475-8191

A = wheelchair accessible   I = interpreter for hearing impaired   F = food   FF = fast food   EF = ethnic food
VF = vegetarian food   RF = regional food   R = restaurants nearby   P = pets welcome   CC = credit cards

Massachusetts

20TH ANNUAL PICKIN' IN THE PINES BLUEGRASS DAY
June (call for exact date)
Look Park, Northampton, MA

Since 1976. Annual attendance is 350 to 600. This Bluegrass Day is eight hours of continuous contemporary and traditional bluegrass music in a beautiful setting of a 200 acre private park. It offers an enjoyable family day with picnicking on the sloping lawn of the theater. Past performers: Smokey Greene, Southern Rail, Northern Lights. Clogging. All performances held outdoors. Hours: noon-8 p.m. Tickets: adults $8, seniors $6, children (under 12) free with adult. A, FF, R, P (on leash), MR, M

Contact: A.B. Acker, Annual Pickin' In The Pines Bluegrass Day, 53 Henry Street, Amherst, MA 01002 • Phone: 413-549-6640

WESTERN NEW ENGLAND OLD-TIME & BLUEGRASS MUSIC CHAMPIONSHIPS
August 18
The Berkshire School, Sheffield, MA

Since 1993. Expected attendance 700. Features an old-time country and bluegrass music contest in a beautiful setting. All funds go to Kiwanis charities. Good family fun. Event held outdoors. Indoor venue in case of rain. Hours: noon-6 p.m. Tickets: $6 adults, $3 youth (10-17 years of age), children under 10 free. A, FF, RF, R, MR, RR, CN, RVN, NH, M

Contact: Paul Kleinwald, P.O. Box 594, Great Barrington, MA 01230 • Phone: 413-528-4252 or 413-528-2553

Michigan

18TH ANNUAL SALT RIVER BLUEGRASS FESTIVAL
July 25-28
Salt River Acres, Oil City, MI

Since 1978. Annual attendance is 1,500 to 2,000. Festival showcases bluegrass and traditional music. It is held at a well-groomed campground with excellent, helpful staff, clean bathrooms, and a children's playground. The stage can accommodate indoor or outdoor shows. Workshops, children's activities, crafts and clogging. The stage show goes on until midnight. There is parking lot picking 24 hours. Tickets: advance $30, at the gate $35. Seniors receive a 20% discount on weekend only.

MR = modern restrooms	RR = rustic restrooms	CO = camping on-site	CN = camping nearby S = hot showers
RVO = RVs on-site	RVN = RVs nearby	HO = hookups on-site	HN = hookups nearby M = motels nearby

Friday $15, Saturday $18, Sunday $10. Advance ticket sales available. A, FF, R, P, MR, RR, CO, S, RVO, HO, M

Contact: George or Kris Carr, Salt River Acres, 775 N. Homer Road, Midland, MI 48640 • Phone: 517-631-7659 or 517-773-5074

ANNUAL WILLOW METRO PARK BLUEGRASS FESTIVAL
June 9
Flat Rock, MI

Since 1980. Annual attendance is 500. Great FREE festival — the only cost is for parking. Features bluegrass and country music with Marcus & Megan (2 Little Fiddlers ages 8-10 years old) showcased this year. All performances held outdoors. A covered area is available for the audience. Hours 6 p.m.-11 p.m. A, F, R, MR, RR, M

Contact: Robert White, Willow Metro Park BG Festival, P.O. Box 5111, Toledo, OH 43611 • Phone: 419-726-5089

IT'S NOT ALMOST IT IS! PARADISE! BLUEGRASS FESTIVAL
October 12-13
Theatre at Mission Point Resort, Mackinac Island, MI

Since 1994. Annual attendance is 300 per day. Features bluegrass, country and gospel music with host band Robert White & The Candy Mountain Express. Past headliners: Larkin Family, Stevens Family, Randall Hylton. All performances held indoors. Hours: Friday 6 p.m.-midnight, Saturday noon-midnight. For a package deal on tickets and room call 1-800-833-7711, and mention the bluegrass festival. Advance weekend tickets $25, both days at the door $30. A, F (restaurant on site), R, Cc, MR, M (on site)

Contact: Robert White, P.O. Box 5111, Toledo, OH 43611 • Phone: 419-726-5089

SOUTHERN MICHIGAN NO. 1 ANNUAL BLUEGRASS FESTIVAL
August 15-18
Wheel Inn Campground, Leslie, MI

Since 1980. Annual attendance is 1,000 to 3,000. Pure and simple bluegrass, country and gospel music. Host band is Robert White & The Candy Mountain Express. Past headliners: Bill Monroe, Mac Wiseman, Jim & Jesse, Country Gentlemen, Osborne Brothers, Lewis Family, Stevens Family, and many, many more. Hillbilly beans, cornbread, biscuits and gravy. Children's activities, crafts area, and clogging. All performances held outdoors. Hours: Thursday 4 p.m.-midnight, Friday and Saturday noon-midnight, Sunday music starts at 1 p.m. Tickets for entire weekend $25 in advance, $35 at gate. Single day prices vary. A, FF, RF, P (not in concert area), RR, CO, S, RVO, RVN, HO, HN, M

Contact: Robert White, P.O. Box 5111, Toledo, OH 43611 • Phone: 419-726-5089

A = wheelchair accessible   I = interpreter for hearing impaired   F = food   FF = fast food   EF = ethnic food
VF = vegetarian food   RF = regional food   R = restaurants nearby   P = pets welcome   CC = credit cards

St. Mary Park Bluegrass Festival
July (call for exact date)
St. Mary Park, Monroe, MI

Since 1981. Annual attendance is 400. This FREE festival features bluegrass, country and gospel music, with "Mr. Bluegrass," Robert White. Children's activities. Performances held both indoors and outdoors. A covered area is available for the audience outdoors. Hours: 6 p.m.-9 p.m. A, R, MR, RR, M

Contact: Robert White, St. Mary Park Bluegrass Festival, P.O. Box 5111, Toledo, OH 43611 • Phone: 419-726-5089

Minnesota

Minnesota Bluegrass & Old-Time Music Festival
August 2-4
Camp in the Woods Resort, Zimmerman, MN

Since 1980. Annual attendance is 5,000. A friendly community atmosphere and lots of campground jamming are what make this festival great. Features bluegrass, old-time string band, and related acoustic music. Past performers: Osborne Brothers, Del McCoury, Chubby Wise, Carolina, Alison Krauss. All performances held outdoors. Workshops, children's activities, crafts area, and dancing (contra and Cajun). Hours: 8 a.m.-11 p.m. daily. Tickets: $12/day, $35/weekend. Advance ticket sales available. A, F (breakfasts and dinners), FF, EF, VF, RF, R, P, CC, RR, CO, S, RVO, M

Contact: Jed Malischke, P.O. Box 480, Spooner, WI 54801 • Phone: 715-635-2479

Money Creek Haven Country-Bluegrass Festival
August 15-18
Money Creek Haven, Houston, MN

Since 1993. Estimated attendance is 1,500. Features acoustic bluegrass (SPBGMA rules apply) mixed with old-time country music. Located in the "scenic bluff country" with a 34 mile bike trail (bicycles for rent at Rushford). This year's headliners include Bob Lewis Family Band, Chapman Family Band, Bluegrass Tradition, Kimmel, Rosenstein & Co. Past performers: Sand Mountain Boys, Vern Young, Shorty & Lorene. Workshops, children's activities and crafts. All performances outdoors. Hours are Thursday, Friday and Saturday 1 p.m.-11 p.m., and Sunday 10 a.m.-5 p.m. A four-day pass is $20 ($15 in advance), a 3-day pass is $16 ($14 in advance). Daily tickets (Thursday, Friday and Sunday) are $6. Saturday tickets are $12, after 5:00 p.m. $8. A, FF, RF, R, P (not in stage area), MR, CO, CN, S, RVO, RVN, HO, HN, M

Contact: Howard Otis, P.O. Box 93, Rushford, MN 55971 • Phone: 800-301-6910

MR = modern restrooms   RR = rustic restrooms   CO = camping on-site   CN = camping nearby   S = hot showers
RVO = RVs on-site   RVN = RVs nearby   HO = hookups on-site   HN = hookups nearby   M = motels nearby

SWAYED PINES FOLK FESTIVAL
April 27 (call to verify)
St. Johns University, Collegeville, MN

Since 1973. Annual attendance is 10,000 to 15,000. Swayed Pines is a family fun-day featuring fiddle music, bluegrass, a variety of traditional folk music, a crafts fair and an assortment of international food. This event fosters an appreciation of traditional music, art and crafts as well as appreciation for the richness of cultural diversity in arts, music and crafts. Fiddle contest, impromptu jam sessions, folk music for afternoon and evening concerts, wandering minstrels. This year's headliner is John McCutcheon. Past performers: Doc Watson, Tom Paxton, Mike Seeger, Tom Chapin, Elizabeth "Libba" Cotton, Garrison Keillor, John McCutcheon, Arlo Guthrie, Greg Brown, Holly Near. Events held both indoors and outdoors; all concerts are indoors. Hours: noon-6 p.m. Concerts at 5 p.m. and 8 p.m. Admission to craft show and fiddle contest is free. Admission charge for the evening concert is $10. Advance ticket sales available. A, FF, EF, R, CC, MR, CN, RVN, M

Contact: Darla Pikkaraine or Lee A. Hanley, P.O. Box 7222, Collegeville, MN 56321 • Phone: 612-363-3249 or 612-363-2596 • Fax: 612-363-3446

Mississippi

ACOUSTIC EXTRAORDINAIRE
March 2
BPOE #599 Lodge Ballroom, Hattiesburg, MS

Since 1993. Annual attendance is 300+. Features bluegrass, gospel and country music with a songwriter/artist concert-in-the-round! This year's headliners: Carl Jackson, Larry Cordle, Jim Rushing, Jerry Sally. All performances held indoors. Doors open at 6 p.m., reception 7 p.m., concert 8 p.m. Tickets are $15 per person. Advance ticket sales available. A, F (finger food at reception), R, MR, CN, S, RVO, RVN, HO, HN, M

Contact: Bertie Sullivan, Elks Dixie Music Committee, P.O. Box 16778, Hattiesburg, MS 39404-6778 • Phone: 601-544-7676 • Fax: 601-582-3850

BANNER BLUEGRASS FESTIVAL
August 9-10
Banner Blount Park, Banner, MS

Since 1990. Annual attendance is 800 to 1,200. Crafts area and clogging. All performances held outdoors. A covered area is available for the audience. Hours: Friday 7-11, Saturday 2-6 and 7-11. Tickets: $14 for the weekend, $7 Friday, $8 Saturday. A, F, R, P (on leash), MR, S, RVO, HO, M

Contact: Jessie E. Davis, P.O. Box 802, Bruce, MS 38915 • Phone: 601-983-2375

A = wheelchair accessible   I = interpreter for hearing impaired   F = food   FF = fast food   EF = ethnic food
VF = vegetarian food   RF = regional food   R = restaurants nearby   P = pets welcome   CC = credit cards

ELKS DIXIE BLUEGRASS FESTIVAL
July 10-13
Elks Dixie Music Park, Hattiesburg, MS

Since 1991. Annual attendance is 5,000 to 6,000. Features bluegrass, acoustic country and gospel music. This family-style bluegrass festival is the state's only multiple day not-for-profit bluegrass event. Collaborates with USM College of the Arts, county government, volunteer firemen, Boy Scouts, Foster Grandparents, Camp Shelby, regional mall and local hospital. This year's headliners: Mac Wiseman, The Charlie Sizemore Band, Sand Mountain Boys, Lickety Split, Thomas Tate & The Countian Bluegrass, and others to be announced. Past performers: Nashville Bluegrass Band, Cox Family, Lonesome River Band, IIIrd Tyme Out, The Reno Brothers, High Strung, Doyle Lawson & Quicksilver, Randy Franks, Foxfire, Rarely Herd. Musical competitions, workshops, children's activities, crafts area, and dancing (clogging). All performances held outdoors. Hours: July 10th 5 p.m. until ??, July 11th 3 p.m. until ??, July 12th and 13th 1 p.m. until ??. Daily admission and/or 4-day pass. Call for details. Advance ticket sales available. A, I, FF, RF, R, P (on leash), MR, CO, CN, S, RVO, RVN, HO, HN, M

Contact: Bertie Sullivan, Elks Dixie Music Committee, P.O. Box 16778, Hattiesburg, MS 39404-6778 • Phone: 601-544-7676 • Fax: 601-582-3850

MISSISSIPPI REGIONAL PIZZA HUT INTERNATIONAL BLUEGRASS SHOWDOWN
April 13
Elks Dixie Music Park, Hattiesburg, MS

Since 1992. Annual attendance is 500+. Held in a natural amphitheatre nestled in a pine forest. The concert stage, although outdoors, is air-conditioned. Talent search is a stepping stone to career enhancing opportunities with favorable exposure. Features acoustic country, bluegrass and folk music. This year's headliner is Lickety Split. Musical competitions. All performances held outdoors. Cajun cuisine. Park opens at 11 a.m. Stage show starts at 3 p.m. Tickets: $10 adults, $5 youth 13-16, children under 12 admitted free. Special pricing for groups of 20 or more; call for details. Advance ticket sales available. A, I, FF, EF, RF, P (on leash), MR, CO, CN, S, RVO, RVN, HO, HN, M

Contact: Bertie Sullivan, International Bluegrass Showdown, P.O. Box 16778, Hattiesburg, MS 39404-6778 • Phone: 601-544-7676 • Fax: 601-582-3850

SOUTH MISSISSIPPI BLUEGRASS JAMBOREE
March 22
South Mississippi Music Hall, Runnelstown, MS

Since 1989. Annual attendance is 750+. Features bluegrass and gospel music. Annual concert of Doyle Lawson for tri-state area of Alabama, Mississippi and Louisiana. This year's headliners: Doyle Lawson & Quicksilver, Steel Blue. All performances

---

MR = modern restrooms   RR = rustic restrooms   CO = camping on-site   CN = camping nearby   S = hot showers
RVO = RVs on-site   RVN = RVs nearby   HO = hookups on-site   HN = hookups nearby   M = motels nearby

held indoors. Hours: 7 p.m. until ??. Doors open at 6 p.m. Tickets: $10 at the door, $8 in advance, preschoolers admitted free. A, FF, RF, R, MR, RVN, M

Contact: Bertie Sullivan, South Mississippi Bluegrass Jamboree, P.O. Box 16778, Hattiesburg, MS 39404-6778 • Phone: 601-544-7676 • Fax: 601-582-3850

SPARKS FAMILY'S 5TH ANNUAL BLUEGRASS FESTIVAL
May 17-18
Co. Rd. 961, 4 1/2 miles west of Belmont, MS

Since 1991. Traditional bluegrass and bluegrass gospel in a warm, friendly atmosphere. All performances held outdoors. A covered area is available for the audience. Hours: Friday 7 p.m. until ??, and Saturday noon to ??. Call for ticket prices. Advance ticket sales available. F, R, MR, S, RVO, HO, M

Contact: Bryan Sparks, 1193 Co. Road 961, Belmont, MS 38827 • Phone: 601-454-7823

THE SPARKS FAMILY'S 13TH ANNUAL BLUEGRASS FESTIVAL
August 3-4
4 1/2 miles west of Belmont, MS

Since 1983. Features bluegrass and gospel music with down-to-earth home folks. Hours are Friday 7:00 p.m.-midnight. Saturday 1 p.m.-11 p.m. Advance ticket sales available. Call for pricing. R, MR, RVO, HO, M

Contact: Bryan Sparks, 1193 Co. Road 961, Belmont, MS 38827 • Phone: 601-454-7823

Missouri

15TH LAND OF MARK TWAIN MUSIC FESTIVAL
November 15-17
Holiday Inn, Hannibal, MO

Since 1982. Annual attendance is 1,500. Features top name bluegrass bands. Workshops, children's activities, crafts area. All performances held indoors. Hours: 9-12. Tickets: $18. A, F (restaurant on site), R, MR, RVN, M

Contact: Delbert Spray, Land of Mark Twain Music Festival, RR 1, Box 71, Kahoka, MO 63445 • Phone: 314-853-4344

A = wheelchair accessible   I = interpreter for hearing impaired   F = food   FF = fast food   EF = ethnic food
VF = vegetarian food   RF = regional food   R = restaurants nearby   P = pets welcome   CC = credit cards

18TH ANNUAL TSBA WINTER BLUEGRASS MUSIC FESTIVAL
February 16-18
Holiday Inn, Hannibal, MO

Since 1978. Annual attendance is 2,000. Features top name bands. Workshops, children's activities, crafts area. All performances held indoors. Hours: 9-12. Tickets: $18. A, F (restaurant on site), R, MR, RVN, M

Contact: Delbert Spray, Annual TSBA Winter Bluegrass Festival, RR 1, Box 71, Kahoka, MO 63445 • Phone: 314-853-4344

DIXON BLUEGRASS PICKIN' TIME
May 23-26, August 29-September 1
Dixon Music Park, Hwy. 133 North, Dixon, MO

Since 1969. Good clean family fun. Workshops and crafts area. All performances outdoors. Good home-cooked food. Call for hours and prices. A, F, R, P, MR, S, RVO, HO

Contact: Bill or Mona Jones, P.O. Box 466, Dixon, MO 65459 • Phone: 314-759-7716

HOBA BLUEGRASS FESTIVAL
June 13-16
HOBA Park, West Plains, MO

Since 1980. Attendance varies. Friendly, family-oriented festival held in a clean, shaded park. Bands and musicians "jam all the time." Features bluegrass music, non-amplified acoustic instruments and clogging. This year's headliners include the Drifters, Kansas City. Past performers include the Sand Mountain Boys. All performances held outdoors. Park opens one week early. Near shopping center. $14 for weekend pass. Also daily prices. A, F (breakfast), FF, R, P, MR, S, RVO, HO, M

Contact: Ethel Willard or Ken Greene, P.O. Box 541, West Plains, MO 65775 • Phone: 417-256-5154

HOBA BLUEGRASS FESTIVAL – HEART OF THE OZARKS
August 8-11
HOBA Park, West Plains, MO

Since 1980. Attendance varies. Friendly, family-oriented festival held in a clean, shaded park. Bands and musicians "jam all the time." Features bluegrass music, non-amplified acoustic instruments and clogging. Specialty is homemade pies. All performances held outdoors. Park opens one week early. Near shopping center. $14 for weekend pass. Also daily prices. A, F (breakfast), FF, R, P, MR, S, RVO, HO, M

Contact: Ethel Willard or Ken Greene, P.O. Box 541, West Plains, MO 65775 • Phone: 417-256-5154

MR = modern restrooms   RR = rustic restrooms   CO = camping on-site   CN = camping nearby   S = hot showers
RVO = RVs on-site   RVN = RVs nearby   HO = hookups on-site   HN = hookups nearby   M = motels nearby

KAHOKA FESTIVAL OF BLUEGRASS MUSIC
August 7-10
Clark County Fairgrounds, Kahoka, MO

Since 1972. Annual attendance is 4,000. Headliners include Sand Mountain Boys, Freddy Clark Family, Bob Lewis Family, Goldwing, and Ozark Lightnin' Cloggers. There is lots of jamming, great stage shows, good bands, and a friendly atmosphere. There are workshops, children's activities, crafts and dancing (clogging). All performances are outdoors. There is a covered area for the audience. Festival hours are 9 a.m.-midnight. Tickets are $25 for the four days. A, FF, RF, R, P, MR, S, RVN, M

Contact: Delbert Spray, Kahoka Festival of Bluegrass Music, RR 1, Box 71, Kahoka, MO 63445 • Phone: 314-853-4344

McCULLOUGH PARK FAMILY BLUEGRASS FESTIVAL
July 17-21, September 4-7
McCullough Park Campground, Highway 65, Chillicothe, MO

Since 1981. Clean, family atmosphere. No alcohol or drugs allowed on grounds. Lots of shade trees. The grounds are mowed, trimmed and sprayed. Fiddle competitions, open and youth. Crafts area. All performances are held outdoors. A 5-day pass is $30, a 4-day pass $25, a 3-day pass $20. A, FF, RF, R, P, MR, CN, S, RVO, RVN, HO, HN, M

Contact: Don or Pat McCullough, 1560 Calhoun, Chillicothe, MO 64601 • Phone: 816-646-2795 or 816-646-2735

PICKIN' BY THE RIVER
August 16-18
Arrowhead Hills Campground, Bollinger County, Grassy, MO

Since 1968. Annual attendance is 800 to 1,200. A great family reunion atmosphere where attendees return year after year. Past performers: Osborne Brothers, Tennessee Gentlemen, Jim & Jesse, Carl Story. All performances held outdoors. Crafts area. Performances Friday night, Saturday afternoon and evening, and Sunday morning. Weekend pass is $25 plus camping. A, FF, R, P, MR, CO, CN, S, RVO, RVN, HO, HN, M (25 mi.)

Contact: Mike or Linda Farmer, Pickin' By The River, HCR 64, Box 700, Grassy, MO 63753 • Phone: 314-495-2204

SALLY MOUNTAIN 10TH ANNUAL BLUEGRASS FESTIVAL
July 3-7
Sally Mountain Park, 3 mi. west of Queen City on Rt. W, MO

Since 1986. Wonderful music, fun and fellowship. Past performers: Lewis Family, Bud Reese, Possum Trot, Bluegrass Brigade, Sally Mountain with Rhonda Vincent. Workshops and children's activities. All performances held outdoors. Hours vary.

A = wheelchair accessible   I = interpreter for hearing impaired   F = food   FF = fast food   EF = ethnic food
VF = vegetarian food   RF = regional food   R = restaurants nearby   P = pets welcome   CC = credit cards

Call for this year's prices. Five-day passes available. Children (12 and under) free. A, FF, RF, R, RR, S, RVO, HO, M

Contact: Johnny Vincent, Rt. 2, Box 15, Greentop, MO 63546 • Phone: 816-949-2345 or 816-766-2522

SNYDER BLUEGRASS FESTIVAL
July 26-27
Snyder Park, Lawrenceburg, MO

Since 1993. Annual attendance is 800. Held in a beautiful park reminiscent of a natural amphitheatre. This festival showcases bluegrass and bluegrass gospel music amidst tall trees along a sloping hillside with the stage near the bottom. Past performers: Alan Munde. All performances held outdoors. Crafts area. Hours: Friday 7-11 p.m., Saturday 1-6 p.m. and 7-11 p.m. Tickets: Friday night $6, Saturday all day $9, Saturday evening only $7. Two-day pass $14. Camping and full hook-up $7. A, FF, R, MR, CO, S, RVO, HO, M

Contact: Virginia Snyder, Snyder Bluegrass Festival, 1347 East Broadmoor, Springfield, MO 65804 • Phone: 417-882-6621

THE GATEWAY CITY BLUEGRASS FESTIVAL
February 23-25
Henry VIII Ramada Hotel, I-70 exit 235B, Lindbergh Blvd, St. Louis, MO

Since 1989. Annual attendance is 3,000. A great lineup of bands is featured at this family festival which is held in conjunction with the Vintage Guitar Show (20 exhibits). This year's headliners: Lonesome River Band, Lewis Family, Dry Branch Fire Squad, Parmley Vestal & Continental Divide, Lynn Morris, and 6 other bands. Past performers: Ralph Stanley, Jim & Jesse, Cox Family, Laurie Lewis, Front Range. Workshops, children's activities and crafts. All performances held indoors. Hours: Friday 7:30 p.m. through Sunday 3:00 p.m. Tickets: weekend pass $25, or each show $10 and up. Children admitted at half price. Advance ticket sales available. A, F, (full service on site), R, MR, S, M (festival held at hotel)

Contact: Terry M. Lease, Downstate Illinois Bluegrass Assoc., P.O. Box 456, Jacksonville, IL 62651 • Phone: 217-243-3159

Montana

BITTERROOT VALLEY BLUEGRASS FESTIVAL
July 13-14
Ravalli County Fairgrounds, Hamilton, MT

Since 1989. Annual attendance is 2,000±. This festival is located in perhaps the most beautiful spot in the Rocky Mountains in the beautiful Bitterroot Mountains.

MR = modern restrooms   RR = rustic restrooms   CO = camping on-site   CN = camping nearby   S = hot showers
RVO = RVs on-site   RVN = RVs nearby   HO = hookups on-site   HN = hookups nearby   M = motels nearby

Lots to do before and after the festival. Also great arts and crafts vendors. Past performers: Special Consensus, Ryestraw, Andy Rau Band, Marc Pruett. Workshops and children's activities. All performances held outdoors. Hours: July 13th 10 a.m.-9 p.m., July 14th 9 a.m.-6:30 p.m. Tickets are $8 per day, $15 for the weekend. A, F, R, P (under control), MR, CO, RVO, RVN, HN, M

Contact: Mark Dickerson, P.O. Box 1371, Hamilton, MT 59840 • Phone: 406-363-5450 • Fax: 406-363-2796

MUSICIANS RENDEZVOUS
July 5-7
Itch Kep Pe Park, Columbus, MT

Since 1990. Annual attendance is 2,000. This festival is situated on the Yellowstone River in the foothills of the Beartooth Mountains. Features bluegrass, old-time fiddle, country and acoustic music. Workshops, children's activities and crafts area. All performances held outdoors. A covered area is available for the audience. Hours: noon-8 p.m. Saturday, noon-6 p.m. Sunday. Tickets: $5 for all three days. A, FF, R, P, MR, RR, CO, RVN, HN, M

Contact: Aron Strange, Musicians Rendezvous, P.O. Box 489, Columbus, MT 59019 • Phone: 406-322-4143 (day) or 406-322-4745 (evening)

New Hampshire

4TH ANNUAL PEMI VALLEY BLUEGRASS FESTIVAL
August 2-4
Branch Brook Campground, Campton, NH

Since 1993. Annual attendance is 2,000. Features acoustic bluegrass music, some old-time country, and lots of field pickin'. Beautiful scenic site in the White Mountains with varied family activities such as river tubing, swimming and fishing with major recreational attractions nearby. AAA-rated, grassy, well-groomed campground. Musical competitions, workshops, children's area, vendors and dancing (clogging). Easy access just off I-93 at Exit 28. Home-cooked food available. Church prepared breakfasts and Saturday supper. This year's headliners: Mac Wiseman, The Lost & Found, Southern Rail, Kevin Williamson & Shadow Ridge, Case Brothers, Smokey Greene. Past performers: Dry Branch Fire Squad, Front Range, Warrior River Boys, Stevens Family. All performances held outdoors. A covered area is available for the audience. Hours: Friday 1-10 p.m., Saturday 9 a.m.-11 p.m., Sunday 9 a.m.-6 p.m. Tickets: 3-day pass before July 15th $28, at gate $34. Friday $10, Saturday all day $18, after 6 p.m. $12. Sunday $12. A, F, FF, R, P ($10 fee; on leash; not allowed in concert area), MR, RR, CO, CN, S, RVO, RVN, HO, HN, M

Contact: Susan & Russell Marsden, Pemi Valley Productions, P.O. Box 658, Campton, NH 03223 • Phone: 603-726-3471

A = wheelchair accessible   I = interpreter for hearing impaired   F = food   FF = fast food   EF = ethnic food
VF = vegetarian food   RF = regional food   R = restaurants nearby   P = pets welcome   CC = credit cards

HAYSEED "MOSTLY" BLUEGRASS FESTIVAL
July 20-21
Dow Strip, Franconia, NH

Since 1981. Annual attendance varies. Features bluegrass, folk, and some gospel, country and blues. All performers play for the benefit of the local fire/police and life squad. The entertainers are not paid, and some of these bands have performed for 15 years! Past performers include Back Porch String Band, Parker Road Bluegrass Band, Tri-State Bluegrass, Silver Dollar String Band, Gopher Broke, and Break For Moose. Children's activities. All performances held outdoors. Hours: noon-6 p.m. daily. Tickets are $6. Children (under 12) free. Advance ticket sales and two-day discount tickets available. A, F, R, RR, CN, RVN, HN, M

Contact: Joel Peabody or David Southworth, Hayseed Bluegrass Festival, Franconia, NH 03580 • Phone: 603-823-8823 or 603-823-5344

New Jersey

25TH ANNUAL DELAWARE VALLEY BLUEGRASS FESTIVAL
August 30-September 1
Salem County Fairgrounds, Woodstown, NJ

Since 1972. Annual attendance is 4,000. The festival focuses on music, quality of artists and perfect sound. There are children's activities and crafts. All performances are held outdoors. There is a covered area for the audience. Hours are Friday 3 p.m.-11 p.m., Saturday noon to midnight, Sunday 10 a.m.-6 p.m. Ticket prices: Friday $20, Saturday $25, Sunday $20. A weekend pass is $60. Advance ticket sales are available. A, F, R, RR, CO, M

Contact: Carl Goldstein or Walt Robbins, Box 3672, Greenville, DE 19807 • Phone: 302-475-3457

4TH OCEAN COUNTY BLUEGRASS FESTIVAL
February 11 (snow date February 18)
Albert Music Hall, Priff School, Rt. 532, Wells Mills Rd., Waretown, NJ

Since 1994. Annual attendance is 400+. Live stage presentations of bluegrass music performed by bluegrass bands from the New Jersey, New York and Pennsylvania regions. All performances are held indoors. Hours: 12:30 to 5 p.m. Adults $8, children $1. A, FF, R, MR, CN, RVN, HN, M

Contact: Pinelands Cultural Society, P.O. Box 657, Waretown, NJ 08758 • Phone: 609-971-1593

MR = modern restrooms   RR = rustic restrooms   CO = camping on-site   CN = camping nearby   S = hot showers
RVO = RVs on-site   RVN = RVs nearby   HO = hookups on-site   HN = hookups nearby   M = motels nearby

5TH OCEAN COUNTY BLUEGRASS FESTIVAL
September 8
Albert Music Hall, Priff School, Rt. 532, Wells Mills Rd., Waretown, NJ

Since 1994. Annual attendance is 400+. Live stage presentations of bluegrass music performed by bluegrass bands from the New Jersey, New York and Pennsylvania regions. All performances are held indoors. Hours: 12:30 to 5 p.m. Adults $8, children $1. A, FF, R, MR, CN, RVN, HN, M

Contact: Pinelands Cultural Society, P.O. Box 657, Waretown, NJ 08758 • Phone: 609-971-1593

HOMEPLACE FESTIVAL
November 10
Albert Music Hall, Priff School, Rt. 532, Wells Mills Rd., Waretown, NJ

Since 1980. Annual attendance is 400+. Features bands from the New Jersey, New York and Pennsylvania regions playing country, bluegrass and traditional music. Musicians from the early days of Albert Music Hall are featured. All performances are held indoors. Hours: 12:30 to 5 p.m. Adults $8, children $1. A, FF, R, MR, CN, RVN, HN, M

Contact: Pinelands Cultural Society, P.O. Box 657, Waretown, NJ 08758 • Phone: 609-971-1593

PINE BARREN'S FESTIVAL
May 5
Albert Music Hall, Priff School, Rt. 532, Wells Mills Rd., Waretown, NJ

Since 1970. Annual attendance is 400+. The Pine Barren's Festival is a celebration dedicated to the New Jersey Pine Barrens. It is an event featuring down-home bluegrass, country and traditional music with bands from the New Jersey, New York and Pennsylvania region. All performances are held indoors. Hours: 12:30 to 5 p.m. Adults $8, children $1. A, FF, R, MR, CN, RVN, HN, M

Contact: Pinelands Cultural Society, P.O. Box 657, Waretown, NJ 08758 • Phone: 609-971-1593

New York

1000 ISLANDS BLUEGRASS FESTIVAL
June 7-9
Captain Clayton's Campgrounds, St. Lawrence River, Clayton, NY

Since 1991. Annual attendance is 900 to 1,000. This is a family-oriented festival in an outdoor setting in the beautiful 1000 Islands area along the St. Lawrence River.

A = wheelchair accessible   I = interpreter for hearing impaired   F = food   FF = fast food   EF = ethnic food
VF = vegetarian food   RF = regional food   R = restaurants nearby   P = pets welcome   CC = credit cards

Internationally known bands plus local and "middle road" bands are brought together for 3 days of great bluegrass music. The audience comes from Ontario and Quebec, Canada, as well as from many of the eastern United States. Considered one of the premier bluegrass festivals on both sides of the border. This year's headliners: U.S. Navy band Country Current, The Stevens Family. Past performers: The Lonesome River Band, Larry Sparks, Mr. B's All-Star Band, Kim Fox, Blue Mule, Gibson Brothers Band. All performances held outdoors. A covered area is available for the audience. Open mic on Friday. Vendors. Two state parks nearby. Hours: Friday 5-10, Saturday 10-11, Sunday 9-4. Call for ticket prices. Advance tickets available. A, FF (some specialty foods), R, MR, RR, CO, CN, S, RVO, RVN, HO, HN, M

Contact: Gerry Kirkey, 1,000 Islands Bluegrass Festival, P.O. Box 195, Clayton, NY 13624 • Phone: 315-686-5385 • Fax: same (call first)

BILL KNOWLTON'S BLUEGRASS RAMBLE PICNIC
August 3-5
Oswego County Fairgrounds, Sandy Creek, NY

Since 1973. Annual attendance is 1,000. This is the oldest bluegrass festival in New York. It is sponsored by the Central New York Bluegrass Association, a nonprofit organization, and features bluegrass and old-time country music. Draws a good Canadian crowd. Past performers: Lee Moore, Larry Sparks, Gary Ferguson, Bob Paisley, Smokey Greene, Don Stover, Salmon River Boys, Tom Wilson & Border Bluegrass, Lynden Lee & The Cherry Valley Boys, Andy Pawlenko & The Smoky Hollow Boys. Friday 6 p.m. open stage. Saturday noon-11 p.m. Sunday 11 a.m.-7 p.m. Call for pricing. Advance sale discount. A, FF, VF, R, P (not in performance area), MR, CO, RVO, RVN, HO, HN, M

Contact: Bill Knowlton, CNY Bluegrass Association, 125 Meyers Road, Liverpool, NY 13088-4449 • Phone: 315-457-6100 or 315-652-5550 (for tickets)

LAZY RIVER BLUEGRASS FESTIVAL
September 20-22
Lazy River Campground, Gardiner, NY

Since 1992. This is a true family bluegrass festival held at a beautiful camping resort. Good bands at a reasonable price. This year's headliner is The Lewis Family. Past performers: Del McCoury, Gilles Brothers, Charlie Cline, Charlie Sizemore, Warrior River Boys, Lost & Found, Sand Mountain Boys. Off stage field picking. All performances held outdoors. A covered area is available for the audience outdoors. Hours: Friday 6 p.m.-10:30 p.m., Saturday 10-10, Sunday 10 a.m.-6:15 p.m. Full weekend tickets: $30 in advance (before September 1st), $35 at the gate. Per day tickets: Friday night $8, Saturday $17, Sunday $14. Children under 12 admitted free.

Contact: Bernie & Marlene Carney, Lazy River Bluegrass Festival, 70 Brenda Lane, Stone Ridge, NY 12484 • Phone: 914-255-5193 or 914-687-9781

MR = modern restrooms   RR = rustic restrooms   CO = camping on-site   CN = camping nearby   S = hot showers
RVO = RVs on-site   RVN = RVs nearby   HO = hookups on-site   HN = hookups nearby   M = motels nearby

PEACEFUL VALLEY BLUEGRASS FESTIVAL

July 18-21
Peaceful Valley Campsite, Catskill Mountains, Shinhopple, NY

Since 1981. Annual attendance is 18,000. Features strictly traditional bluegrass music. Held in a beautiful location along a river with great sound. This year's headliners include Jim & Jesse, Lewis Family, Chubby Wise, Stevens Family, Larkin Family and a total of 21 bands. All performances held outdoors under large tented areas. Workshops, children's activities, crafts area and dancing (square and clogging). Hours: 10 a.m.-midnight. Call for ticket prices. Advance ticket sales available. A, F, R, CC, MR, RR, CO, CN, S, RVO, RVN, HO, HN, M

Contact: Arnold Baker, Peaceful Valley Promotions, Inc., HC 89, Box 56, Downsville, NY 13755 • Phone: 607-363-2211 • Fax: 607-363-2028

PINES BLUEGRASS FESTIVAL

March 14-17
Pines Hotel, South Fallsburg, NY

Since 1986. Annual attendance 1,000. This early spring festival is held indoors and features strictly bluegrass music. This year's headliners: Del McCoury, Lewis Family, Raymond Fairchild, and 11 other bands. Workshops, children's activities, crafts area and dancing (squares and clogging). Hours: 10 a.m.-midnight each day. Call for ticket prices. Advance ticket sales available. A, F (included with price of tickets), R, CC, MR, M

Contact: Arnold Banker, Peaceful Valley Promotions, Inc., HC 89, Box 56, Downsville, NY 13755 • Phone: 607-363-2211 or 914-434-6000 • Fax: 607-363-2028

RICK & CAROL'S COUNTRY MUSIC & BLUEGRASS FESTIVAL

July 26-27
Patten Mills Road, off Route 149, W. Fort Ann, NY

Since 1985. Annual attendance is 200 to 400. This is a small, family-run event with all-night parking lot pickers and grinners! Restaurant on the premises specializing in homestyle meals. Smokey Greene is a featured artist each year. All performances held outdoors. A covered area is available for the audience. Hours: Saturday noon-midnight, Sunday 10 a.m.-6 p.m. Tickets: $20 in advance for both days, $15 at gate for Saturday, $10 at gate for Sunday. A, F (homestyle), R (on property), MR, CO, RVN, M

Contact: Carol Twiss, RR 1, Box 1273, Fort Ann, NY 12827 • Phone: 518-793-8987

A = wheelchair accessible   I = interpreter for hearing impaired   F = food   FF = fast food   EF = ethnic food
VF = vegetarian food   RF = regional food   R = restaurants nearby   P = pets welcome   CC = credit cards

St. Lawrence Valley Bluegrass Festival
August 16-18
Fairgrounds, Rock Island St., Gouverneur, NY

Since 1990. Lots of campground picking. International crowd (Canadian and US). This year's headliners: MC Mike O'Reilly and his new band (Dick Smith, Bob Goff, Ray Legere), Case Brothers, The Larkin Family. All performances held outdoors. A covered area is available for the audience. Crafts area and swimming pool available. Round-the-clock stages (26-30 hours). Tickets: $20 advance; $25 at the gate. A, F, R, P, MR, RVO, HO (limited), M (limited)

Contact: Bobbe Erdman, St. Lawrence Valley Bluegrass Festival, 5625 State Highway 812, Ogdensburg, NY 13669 • Phone: 315-393-4531

Winterhawk Bluegrass Festival
July 18-21
Rothvoss Farm, Ancramdale, NY

Since 1982. Annual attendance is 3,000±. Winterhawk features an outstanding children's tent with activities all day long. It strongly supports and encourages the appreciation of bluegrass music among children and youth. Workshops are conducted by festival performers. Each year the festival awards a scholarship to a student with an interest or family background in bluegrass music. Applications can be obtained upon request. This year's host band is Dry Branch Fire Squad. Past performers: Alison Krauss, Seldom Scene, Peter Rowan, Tim & Mollie O'Brien. Musical competitions, crafts area, teen dances and square dances. All performances held outdoors. Hours: 10:30 a.m.-midnight. Last year's ticket prices (call to confirm this year's prices): Early bird special (until April 10) $55 for 4 days including camping; 4/10 to 7/1 $65; at gate $70. FF, EF, VF, RF, R, CC, CO, CN, S, M

Contact: Wilma Thomason, Winterhawk Bluegrass Festival, P.O. Box 161, Tremont City, OH 45372 • Phone: 513-390-6211 • Fax: same (call first)

Wrench Wranch Bluegrass Roundup
August 30-September 1
Wrench Wranch, Coventryville, NY

Since 1983. Annual attendance is 1,000. This festival offers a family atmosphere in a scenic area with olde tyme country and bluegrass music for all to enjoy. This year's headliner: Smokie Greene. Other performers (past and present) include Plexigrass, Fish 'n Friends, Dyer Switch. Crafts area and a square dance on Friday night. Performances are both indoors and outdoors, with an outdoor covered area for the audience. Hours: Friday 6 p.m. until ??; Saturday 10 a.m.-11 p.m.; Sunday 10 a.m.-11 p.m. Admission: $15 for weekend, $8 Saturday and Sunday, $5 Friday night. Advance ticket sales available. A, FF, R, P, MR, CO, M

Contact: Ted Wrench, Box 47, RD #1, Bainbridge, NY 13733 • Phone: 607-639-1371

MR = modern restrooms   RR = rustic restrooms   CO = camping on-site   CN = camping nearby   S = hot showers
RVO = RVs on-site   RVN = RVs nearby   HO = hookups on-site   HN = hookups nearby   M = motels nearby

North Carolina

3RD ANNUAL SUNDAY AFTERNOON BLUEGRASS FESTIVAL
October 6
Bond Park Amphitheater, Cary, NC

Since 1994. Annual attendance is 300 to 500. A free Sunday afternoon of great bluegrass music in a comfortable setting featuring fine local bands – with an absolutely great sound system. This year's headliners: Swift Run, The Sunny South Bluegrass Band. Past performers: Craig Smith, Swift Run, ASH&W, The Sunny South Bluegrass Band. All performances held outdoors. Rain venue available. Hours: 1:30 p.m.–6:30 p.m. Admission is free. A, FF, R, P, RR, M

Contact: Mike Acquesta, 8700 Foggy Bottom Drive, Raleigh, NC 27613 • Phone: 919-848-0573 • Fax: 919-783-7642

14TH ANNUAL CHEROKEE BLUEGRASS FESTIVAL
August 22–24
Happy Holiday Campground, Cherokee, NC

Since 1982. Family entertainment and top bluegrass bands. Past performers: Bill Monroe, Osborne Brothers, Jim & Jesse, Lewis Family. All performances held outdoors. A covered area is available for the audience. Crafts area. Hours: noon–11 p.m. daily. Call for ticket information. Advance ticket sales available. A, FF, R, CC, MR, RR, CN, S, RVO, RVN, HO, HN, M

Contact: Norman Adams or Tony Anderson, P.O. Box 98, 112 N. Park Street, Dahlonega, GA 30533 • Phone: 706-864-7203 • Fax: 706-864-1037

69TH ANNUAL MOUNTAIN DANCE & FOLK FESTIVAL
August 1–3
Asheville Civic Center, Asheville, NC

Since 1927. Annual attendance is 2,500 per night. This is the oldest folk festival in the nation. It is a fast-paced celebration of mountain life and lore. Each night is a full show as string bands vie for awards and dance teams twirl and stomp the traditional figures of the Appalachian square dance. Featured are bluegrass and old-time music, ballads and storytelling. Musical competitions, workshops, children's activities, Appalachian crafts and folk/traditional dancing (clogging and smooth). Past performers include David Holt, Cockman Family, Zack Allen, Shapenote Singers. All performances are held indoors. Hours are 7 p.m.–11 p.m. Ticket prices: Thursday $7, Friday $7, Saturday $9. Advance sales available. A, FF, R, CC, MR, CN, RVN, HN, M

Contact: Vickie Hensley or Stewart Canter, Ashville Chamber of Commerce, P.O. Box 1010, Asheville, NC 28802-1010 • Phone: 704-258-6107 or 800-257-5583 • Fax: 704-254-6054

A = wheelchair accessible   I = interpreter for hearing impaired   F = food   FF = fast food   EF = ethnic food
VF = vegetarian food   RF = regional food   R = restaurants nearby   P = pets welcome   CC = credit cards

Asheville Bluegrass Under The Stars
March 1-2
Great Smokies Holiday Inn Sunspree Resort, Asheville, NC

This is the first year for this exciting festival featuring live performances from the upper echelon of bluegrass entertainment in a comfortable indoor setting. This is a chance to rub elbows with "the finest bluegrass musicians on the planet." This year's headliners: Doyle Lawson & Quicksilver, Lou Reid, Terry Baucom & Carolina, IIIrd Tyme Out, Lonesome River Band, Del McCoury Band, Tony Rice. Workshops, children's activities and dancing. Hours: Friday 1-4 p.m. and 8 p.m.-midnight; Saturday 1-5 p.m. and 8 p.m.-midnight. Advance tickets $50 for both days; at the door $60 for both days. A, F (chef prepared hotel food), R, MR, RVN, HN, M

Contact: Milton Harkey, P.O. Box 7661, Asheville, NC 28802-7661 • Phone: 704-252-1233 • Fax: 704-251-2583

Bass Mountain Music Park's Annual Labor Day Festival
August 30-September 1
Bass Mountain Music Park, Highway 49, Burlington, NC

Family-style bluegrass festival. Includes free camping with weekend ticket. Twenty-four hour security. Great home-cooked food. Strings and supplies, arts, crafts and instruments. No alcohol. Past performers: Chubby Wise, Boys From Indiana, Traditional Grass, Reno Brothers, Goins Brothers, Lost & Found, Heritage, New Classic Grass, Shady Grove Band, Bass Mountain Boys, Josh Graves & Kenny Baker, The Churchmen. All performances held outdoors. Hours: Friday 3 p.m.-midnight; Saturday 11 a.m.-midnight; Sunday 11 a.m.-6 p.m. Advance 3-day tickets $40; at gate $50. Friday $20, Saturday $20, Sunday $10. $5 senior citizen discount. A, FF, EF, VF, RF, R, P (on leash), RR, CO, S, RVO, M

Contact: John Maness, 2233 Bellemont-Alamance Road, Burlington, NC 27215 • Phone: 910-228-7344 • Fax: 910-228-7305

Bass Mountain Music Park's Annual Memorial Day Festival
May 23-26
Bass Mountain Music Park, Highway 49, Burlington, NC

Family-style bluegrass festival. Includes free camping with weekend ticket. Twenty-four hour security. Great home-cooked food. Strings and supplies, arts, crafts and instruments. No alcohol. Past performers: Chubby Wise, Boys From Indiana, Traditional Grass, Reno Brothers, Goins Brothers, Lost & Found, Heritage, New Classic Grass, Shady Grove Band, Bass Mountain Boys, Josh Graves & Kenny Baker, The Churchmen. All performances held outdoors. Call for hours and prices. Advance ticket sales available. A, FF, EF, VF, RF, R, P (on leash), RR, CO, S, RVO, M

MR = modern restrooms   RR = rustic restrooms   CO = camping on-site   CN = camping nearby   S = hot showers
RVO = RVs on-site   RVN = RVs nearby   HO = hookups on-site   HN = hookups nearby   M = motels nearby

Contact: John Maness, 2233 Bellemont-Alamance Road, Burlington, NC 27215
• Phone: 910-228-7344 • Fax: 910-228-7305

BUTTERWOOD BLUEGRASS FESTIVAL

October 4-6
Butterwood Farm, 12 mi. south of Roanoke Rapids, Littleton, NC

Since 1993. Annual attendance 2,000. Held on 60 acres of scenic beauty, clean, lots of room, family-oriented, very friendly people, well secured. Features strictly traditional bluegrass music. Past performers: Bill Monroe, Osborne Brothers, Lewis Family, Cox Family, Stevens Family, Jim & Jesse, IIIrd Tyme Out. All performances held outdoors. Crafts area and clogging. Hours: Friday and Saturday 11-11, Sunday 11-3. Tickets: Friday $20, Saturday $20, Sunday $7. Three-day advance pass $40. A, FF, RF, R, P, RR, CO, S, RVN, HN, M

Contact: Gail Fox, Rt. 1, Box 448, Littleton, NC 27850 • Phone: 919-586-2230

DOYLE LAWSON AND QUICKSILVER'S BLUEGRASS FESTIVAL

July 11-14
Denton Farm Park, Denton, NC

Since 1981. This event has the chemistry of the old time bluegrass festival as well as all three styles of bluegrass music. Many bluegrass pickers and jam sessions 24-hours a day, and many great historical bluegrass reunions (i.e. Country Gentlemen 1971). This year's headliners: Doyle Lawson & Quicksilver, IIIrd Tyme Out, Lonesome River Band, Bill Monroe. Past performers: Alison Krauss & Union Station, Nashville Bluegrass Band. Musical competitions, workshops, children's activities and crafts area. All performances held outdoors. A covered area is available for the audience. Hours: 9 a.m.-midnight each day. Call for ticket prices. Advance ticket sales available. A, FF, EF, VF, RF, P, MR, CO, S, RVO, HO, M

Contact: Milton Harkey, P.O. Box 7661, Asheville, NC 28802-7661 • Phone: 704-252-1233 • Fax: 704-251-2583

FALL JAMBOREE

September 7-8
Sloan Park, Millbridge, Rowan County, NC

Since 1986. Annual attendance is 4,000 to 5,000. Features bluegrass, traditional, folk, old-time and gospel music with a continuous stage show. Kerr Mill, an 1800's grist mill with a water wheel, is in the park. Visitors can tour the mill and see the old machinery. Hand-cranked ice cream and freshly squeezed lemonade are available. Additional highlights: children's playground in the park, children's activities, crafts and clog dancing. Past performers include Deb & Moon Mullins (Ozark Folk Center), Laura Boosinger, Regional Pizza Hut Bluegrass Band winners and more. All performances are held outdoors. Festival hours are Saturday 10 a.m.-9 p.m., and Sunday 1 p.m.-6 p.m. There is no charge for admission. A, FF, MR, CO, RVO, RVN, HN, M

A = wheelchair accessible   I = interpreter for hearing impaired   F = food   FF = fast food   EF = ethnic food
VF = vegetarian food   RF = regional food   R = restaurants nearby   P = pets welcome   CC = credit cards

Contact: Jack Hodges, 613 Maupin Avenue, Salisbury, NC 28144 • Phone: 704-636-7170

MERLE FEST '96
April 25-28
"Doc" & Merle Watson Stage
Wilkes Community College, Wilkesboro, NC

Since 1988. Annual attendance is 38,000. The "Acoustic Event of the Year," and the fastest growing, hottest festival on the east coast. Songwriting, Heritage craftsmen, storytelling, Little Picker's area, midnight jam, traditional music and dance stage, Sunday morning gospel sing, homespun learning stage, finger style workshops, "Doc" Watson Guitar Contest, Banjo Contest, food vendors, music vendors, and commercial vendors. A documentary of the festival was made by North Carolina public television in 1992 called "Pickin' for Merle," and is being shown nationwide. The festival features roots-oriented traditional music, bluegrass, country, folk, gospel, storytelling and songwriting in a clean, family atmosphere. Doc Watson is this year's host. Past headliners: Emylou Harris, Ricky Skaggs, Mary Chapin Carpenter, Jerry Douglas, Seldom Scene, Tony Rice, and over 100 other artists. Musical competitions, workshops, children's activities, crafts and dancing (folk, ethnic and traditional). Performances held both indoors and outdoors. Gates open 3 p.m. April 25th until midnight. April 26-27 gates open 7 a.m. until midnight. Festival ends April 28 at 8 p.m. Special early bird prices as well as 3-day, 4-day, and individual day tickets – prices vary. Advance tickets available. A, FF, VF, RF, R, CC, MR, RR, CN, RVO, RVN

Contact: Brenda Shepherd, Coordinator, Merle Fest, P.O. Box 120, Wilkesboro, NC 28697 • Phone: 910-838-6291 • Fax: 910-838-6277

OLE TIME FIDDLER'S & BLUEGRASS FESTIVAL
May 24-26
Fiddler's Grove Campground, Union Grove, NC

Since 1924. Annual attendance is 3,500. This is the oldest event of its kind in the United States. Held annually on Memorial Day Weekend, the tradition began in 1924 and is still preserving the heritage of the traditional music and related arts. The Ole Time Fiddler's & Bluegrass Festival brings families and musicians together as they share their common love of traditional old time and bluegrass music. Features the very best old time and bluegrass bands and individuals in competition. Excellent workshop leaders and master fiddlers. This year showcases David Holt and Green Grass Cloggers. Children's activities and music vendors. Traditional clog dancing. All performances held outdoors. Hours: Friday 7 p.m.-11:30 p.m., Saturday 9:30 a.m.-12:30 p.m. and 1 p.m.-12:30 a.m., Sunday 10 a.m.-4:30 p.m. Tickets: $40 (adults, entire festival), $20 (youth, 8-15 yrs., entire festival), under 8 years old admitted free. Advance ticket sales available. A (indoors only, will try to accommodate), FF, RF, R, MR, CO, S, RVO, HO, M

Contact: Harper A. Van Hoy, Ole Time Fiddler's & Bluegrass Festival, P.O. Box 11, Union Grove, NC 28689 • Phone: 704-539-4417

MR = modern restrooms   RR = rustic restrooms   CO = camping on-site   CN = camping nearby   S = hot showers
RVO = RVs on-site   RVN = RVs nearby   HO = hookups on-site   HN = hookups nearby   M = motels nearby

STAR FIDDLER'S CONVENTION
February 24
East Montgomery High School, Biscoe, NC

Since 1926. Annual attendance is 800 to 1,000. This is the oldest and longest running Fiddler's Convention in North Carolina. It features strictly bluegrass and old-time music. Musical competitions and buck dancing. All performances are held indoors. Hours: 7 p.m. to ??. Tickets: adults $6, children (ages 6-12) $2. A, FF, R, MR, CN (approx. 30 miles north and south), M

Contact: Jean Sullivan, Star Fiddler's Convention, P.O. Box 101, Star, NC 27356 • Phone: 910-428-2972

UNION GROVE MUSIC FESTIVAL
August 24
Fiddler's Grove Campground, Union Grove, NC

Since 1988. Annual attendance is 1,000. One of the goals of this festival to to preserve our musical heritage of grass-roots music by promoting families who have kept the tradition alive. It features local families who have handed down old time and bluegrass music from one generation to another. It also showcases the champions from the Ole Time Fiddler's & Bluegrass Festival with an afternoon and evening of excellent entertainment. Performances held both indoors and outdoors. Children's activities. Hours: 1 p.m. to 11:00 p.m. Tickets: adults $8, youth (8 to 15) $5, under 8 admitted free. A (indoors only; try to accommodate otherwise), FF, R, MR, CO, S, RVO, HO, M

Contact: Harper A. Van Hoy, Union Grove Music Festival P.O. Box 11, Union Grove, NC 28689 • Phone: 704-539-4417

North Dakota

ANNUAL MISSOURI RIVER BLUEGRASS & OLD TIME MUSIC FESTIVAL
August 31-September 1
Cross Ranch State Park, near Washburn, ND

Since 1990. Annual attendance is 1,800. Features bluegrass, old-time, country, accordian music, etc. The stage area at Cross Ranch State Park is in a beautiful wooded area. The event is very family oriented with children engaged in fun activities, allowing parents and guardians to enjoy the main stage entertainment. Past performers include Cox Family, Stoney Lonesome, Wheel Hoss, Jerusalem Ridge, and Cantrells. Workshops and crafts. All performances held outdoors. Hours are 11 a.m.-9:30 p.m. Tickets are $7 per day. Children (12 and under) are free. A two-day pass is $13. A, FF, MR, CO, RVO, CN, RVN, M

A = wheelchair accessible   I = interpreter for hearing impaired   F = food   FF = fast food   EF = ethnic food
VF = vegetarian food   RF = regional food   R = restaurants nearby   P = pets welcome   CC = credit cards

Contact: John Andrus, 201 25th Street NW, Minot, ND 58703 • Phone: 701-838-1061

Ohio

2ND ANNUAL BLUEGRASS IN LUXURY
RALPH STANLEY'S BIRTHDAY CELEBRATION
March 29-30
Holiday Inn, Hudson, OH

Since 1995. This is Ralph Stanley's birthday celebration. Everyone can have a piece of Ralph's birthday cake and sign his birthday card! This year's headliners: Ralph Stanley (of course!), Goins Brothers, Jim & Jesse, Bluegrass Mountaineers. All performances held indoors. Children's activities. Hours: Friday 2 p.m.-midnight, Saturday noon-midnight. Tickets: $12-$15. Advance ticket sales available. A, F (restaurant on site), FF, R, MR, CO, S, M (held at Holiday Inn)

Contact: Larry Efaw, Annual Bluegrass in Luxury, 894 Oregon Avenue, Akron, OH 44314-2018 • Phone: 216-753-1543 or 216-644-0255

20TH ANNUAL BLUEGRASS FESTIVAL
August 23-25
Funny Farm Campground, Pioneer, OH

Since 1976. Annual attendance is 2,000. Bluegrass music is enjoyed in a scenic, peaceful, family campground with entertainment for all ages. Past performers: Larry Sparks and the Lonesome Ramblers, Chapman Family, Little Fiddlers. Clogging. All performances held outdoors. A covered area is available for the audience. Hours are all weekend long. Tickets are $22 per person at the gate. Advance ticket sales available. FF, R, P, MR, CO, CN, S, RVO, RVN, HO, HN, M

Contact: William O. Clements, Jr., 19452 Co. Road 12, Pioneer, OH 43554 • Phone: 419-737-2467

AIRPORT GOSPEL BLUEGRASS '96
June 21-22
Dayton-New Lebanon Airport, Dayton, OH

Since 1990. Annual attendance is 600 to 800. Truly a good family-oriented bluegrass gospel sing. Lots of free camping with all-night picking, fun, food and fellowship. Past headliners: Larry Sparks, Upper Room, Principles, Mullins Family. All performances held indoors. Friday 5-11. Saturday 11-10. Admission is free. A, FF, R, MR, RR, CO, CN, RVN, HN, M

Contact: Clyde & Lynn Mullins, 1334 N. Lutheran Church Rd., Dayton, OH 45427 • Phone: 513-854-1406 • Fax: 513-854-6900

MR = modern restrooms   RR = rustic restrooms   CO = camping on-site   CN = camping nearby   S = hot showers
RVO = RVs on-site   RVN = RVs nearby   HO = hookups on-site   HN = hookups nearby   M = motels nearby

Bluegrass Classic at Frontier Ranch

July 25-27

Frontier Ranch, Columbus, OH

> Since 1969. Features reunions and special acts not available at other festivals. Showcases bluegrass and acoustic music. Past performers: Earl Scruggs, Ricky Skaggs, Marty Stuart, Emmy Lou Harris, Sam Bush, Bela Fleck. Workshops and children's activities. Folk and traditional dancing. All performances held outdoors. A covered area is available for the audience. Hours: July 25th, 4 p.m.-midnight, 26th 3 p.m.-midnight, 27th 12-12. Tickets (subject to change): $50 in advance for the entire weekend, $60 at the gate (includes camping). Single days: $20 Thursday, $25 Friday, $25 Saturday, $20 Sunday. A, FF, EF, VF, RF, R, P (on leash at campsite), CC, MR, RR, RVO, M

> Contact: Darrel Adkins, Bluegrass Classic at Frontier Ranch, 1434 South 3B's and K Road, Galena, OH 43021 • Phone: 614-548-4199 • Fax: 614-548-4948

Bluegrass Festival & Children's Fall Festival

October 5

Sauder Farm and Craft Village, Archbold, OH

> Since 1978. Annual attendance is 2,000. Features two bluegrass concerts held during the afternoon in air-conditioned Founder's Hall at the Sauder Farm and Craft Village. For one low admission price, guests can enjoy top-notch bluegrass performers as well as tour the adjacent living-history village. A fun-filled day for the whole family! Past performers include: Full House, County Line Power Company, Foster Family String Band, Northwest Territory. Hours: 10 a.m.-5 p.m. Tickets: $9 adults, $8.50 seniors, $4.50 students (6-16). Group discounts available. - call for information. A, F, R, MR, CN, S, RVO, RVN, HO, HN, M

> Contact: Carolyn Sauder, Bluegrass Festival, 22611 St. Rt. 2, P.O. Box 235, Archbold, OH 43502 • Phone: 800-590-9755 • Fax: 419-445-5251

Bluegrass Get-A-Way

February 16-17

Holiday Inn Hotel & Resort, Fremont & Port Clinton Road, Fremont, OH

> Hear down-home, real bluegrass music at this friendly festival. Headliners include: Lost & Found, The Little Fiddlers, Robert White & The Candy Mountain Express. All performances indoors. Hours and ticket prices to be announced. Advance ticket sales available. A, F (restaurant at site), R, MR, RVN, HN, M (on site)

> Contact: Robert White, Bluegrass Get-A-Way, P.O. Box 5111, Toledo, OH 43611 • Phone: 419-726-5089

A = wheelchair accessible   I = interpreter for hearing impaired   F = food   FF = fast food   EF = ethnic food
VF = vegetarian food   RF = regional food   R = restaurants nearby   P = pets welcome   CC = credit cards

BLUEGRASS PRIMETIME PRE-HOLIDAY FESTIVAL
November 16-17
Holiday Inn Holidome, 5 miles N. of Ohio Turnpike, Sandusky, OH

In its first year, this new festival features bluegrass gospel and country music highlighted by its host band, Robert White & The Candy Mountain Express. Children's activities and crafts area. All performances held indoors. Hours: noon to midnight. Ticket prices to be announced. Advance ticket sales available. A, R, MR, RVN, HN, M

Contact: Robert White, Bluegrass Primetime Pre-Holiday Festival, P.O. Box 5111, Toledo, OH 43611 • Phone: 419-726-5089

COUNTRY STAGE BLUEGRASS FESTIVAL
May 17-18, August 16-17, September 20-21
Country Stage Music Park, County Line Rd. 40, Nova, OH

Since 1991. Annual attendance is 2,500. Traditional and modern bluegrass is performed on 60 acres of well-maintained grounds. Past performers: Gary Brewer & The Kentucky Ramblers, Tony Hickman & Harbourtown. Children's activities, crafts area, and traditional dancing. All performances are held outdoors. A covered area is available for the audience. The music begins on Friday at 6 p.m. and on Saturday at 12 noon. Tickets: $18 for the weekend; $12 for Saturday, $8 for Friday. Advance tickets and seniors $15. Children (under 15) free. A, FF, R, P, MR, RR, S, RVO, RVN, HN, M

Contact: Dona Chambers, 34 Tilton Street, Greenwich, OH 44837 • Phone: 419-752-6881

FIDDLE FEST '96
June 8
Wayne Center for the Arts, Wooster, OH

Since 1984. Annual attendance is 500. Features Old Time Traditional Country and Bluegrass music. Past performers include Byron Berline, John Hartford, Vassar Clements, Johnny Gimble, and Eddie Stubbs. Headliners for this year's Stars of Evening Performance are Kenny Baker and Josh Graves. Committed to keeping old time fiddling music alive. Each year the festival features one of America's top fiddlers, and hosts workshops with "big name" entertainers. Festival hours: 11 a.m.-11 p.m. All events are free except for the evening performance which is $8. Advance ticket sales available. Music competitions, workshops, Appalachian clog dancing, and crafts featuring woodcarving, weaving, quilting and pottery. All performances are held outdoors. A, MR, FF, R, CC, RVN, HN, M

Contact: Roberta Looney, Fiddle Fest '96, 237 S. Walnut Street, Wooster, OH 44691 • Phone: 216-264-2787 • Fax: 216-264-9314

MR = modern restrooms   RR = rustic restrooms   CO = camping on-site   CN = camping nearby   S = hot showers
RVO = RVs on-site   RVN = RVs nearby   HO = hookups on-site   HN = hookups nearby   M = motels nearby

FIRST NIGHT OUT
December 31
Downtown, Toledo, OH

Since 1991. Annual attendance is 10,000 to 15,000. Features bluegrass, country and gospel music. All performances held indoors. Music is from 6 p.m.-midnight. Tickets are $5. A, R, MR, M

Contact: Robert White, First Night Out, P.O. Box 5111, Toledo, OH 43611 • Phone: 419-726-5089

MAPLE CITY BLUEGRASS FESTIVAL
June 21-22
Huron County Fairgrounds, Norwalk, OH

Since 1992. Annual attendance is 300. Huron County is peaceful and quiet, and a bluegrass festival has turned out to be the perfect event for the easy going folk of this area. The festival features bluegrass and bluegrass gospel music. Workshops, children's activities, crafts area, and traditional dancing. All performances held outdoors. An indoor venue is available in case of rain. Hours: Friday 7-12, Saturday 12-12. The park opens on Wednesday. Tickets: Friday $8, Saturday $12, weekend pass $18, plus electric $3 per day. A, F (full kitchen), FF, R, P, MR, CO, S, RVO, HO, M

Contact: Don Cordle or Hershal Cordle, Maple City Bluegrass Festival, 11016 Humm Road, Berlin Heights, OH 44814 • Phone: 419-663-8660 or 419-588-3503 • Fax: 419-588-3503

MOHICAN BLUEGRASS FESTIVAL
September 13-15
Mohican Wilderness Center, 10 mi. south of Loudonville, OH

Since 1992. Annual attendance is 2,000+. A classy, intimate festival with an unsurpassed stage (30' x 30' x 25'). Exceptional music, excellent sound, and gorgeous campsites (80' x 120'). All on six hundred acres with two miles of the Mohican River running through it. Features conventional and progressive bluegrass music. Past performers: Bill Monroe, Tim O'Brien, Jerry Douglas, Ralph Stanley, Seldom Scene, Del McCoury, Lewis Family, Kukuruza, Tony Rice, Osborne Brothers, Claire Lynch and the Front Porch String Band, Lonesome River Band, Dry Branch Fire Squad. All performances held outdoors. Plenty of other great activities in addition to the music including canoeing, tubing, kayaking, mini-golf, swimming, bicycles, playgrounds, hay rides, and day care for children three and older. Square dancing. Friday 5-11, Saturday 11-11, Sunday 11-5. Advance tickets: weekend $34, Friday $12, Saturday $18, Sunday $10. At the gate: weekend $42, Friday $14, Saturday $22, Sunday $12. A, FF, R, P, CC, MR, S, RVO, HO, M

Contact: Ken Wobbecke, Mohican Wilderness Inc., 22462 Wally Road, Glenmont, OH 44628 • Phone: 614-599-6741 or 614-599-5466

A = wheelchair accessible   I = interpreter for hearing impaired   F = food   FF = fast food   EF = ethnic food
VF = vegetarian food   RF = regional food   R = restaurants nearby   P = pets welcome   CC = credit cards

NORTHEASTERN OHIO BLUEGRASS FESTIVAL
July 18-20
Paradise Lakes Family Campground, Bristolville, OH

Since 1988. Features family bluegrass entertainment in a well-organized environment. This year's headliners: Doyle Lawson & Quicksilver, Ralph Stanley, Jim & Jesse, Lewis Family. All performances held outdoors. A covered area is available for the audience. Children's activities, crafts area and dancing. Hours: Thursday 6 p.m.-??, Friday 3 p.m.-midnight, Saturday noon-midnight. Tickets: $8-$14 per day; $30 three-day pass in advance, $35 three-day pass at gate. A, F, R, P, MR, RR, CO, S, RVO, HO, M

Contact: Larry Efaw, Northeastern Ohio Bluegrass Festival, 894 Oregon Avenue, Akron, OH 44314-2018 • Phone: 216-753-1543 or 216-644-0255

WINTER FESTIVAL BLUEGRASS IN SUPER CLASS
January 19-20
Holiday Inn, French Quarters, Perrysburg, OH

Since 1990. Annual attendance is 2,000. Features bluegrass and bluegrass gospel music along with good food and good accommodations. This year's headliners: Osborne Brothers, Ralph Stanley, Lewis Family, Robert White & The Candy Mountain Express, Stephen Family. Past performers: Jim & Jesse, Bill Monroe, Bluegrass Cardinals, Del McCoury, Lost & Found. Children's activities and crafts area. All performances held indoors. Music starts on Friday at noon and on Saturday at 11 a.m. Reserved seating (1-400) $35 in advance, $40 at the door. General admission $35 in advance, $30 at the door. If reserving rooms, be sure to mention the festival. A, F (restaurant on site), R, M (on site)

Contact: Robert White, Winter Festival Bluegrass in Super Class, P.O. Box 5111, Toledo, OH 43611 • Phone: 419-726-5089 or 419-874-3111 (for room reservations)

Oklahoma

SANDERS FAMILY BLUEGRASS FESTIVAL
June 5-8
Sanders Park, McAlester, OK

Since 1976. Annual attendance is 5,000. Good family entertainment. This year's headliners: Osborne Brothers, Lewis Family, Mac Wiseman, Doyle Lawson & Quicksilver. Past performers: Bill Monroe, Ralph Stanley. All performances held outdoors. Call for hours and prices. A, F, R, P, MR, S, RVO, RVN, HO, HN, M

Contact: Freddie Sanders, Sanders Family Bluegrass Festival, Rt. 6, Box 15, McAlester, OK 74501 • Phone: 918-423-4891 • Fax: same (call first)

MR = modern restrooms   RR = rustic restrooms   CO = camping on-site   CN = camping nearby   S = hot showers
RVO = RVs on-site   RVN = RVs nearby   HO = hookups on-site   HN = hookups nearby   M = motels nearby

Oregon

MYRTLE CREEK BLUEGRASS FESTIVAL
September 28-29
Millsite Park, Myrtle Creek, OR

Since 1993. Annual attendance is 5,000. A family-oriented fall music and arts festival with great facilities, crafts, food, kids' activities, workshops, jam sessions, horse-drawn carriage rides, wonderful music and camping. Past performers: Richard Greene, Rose Maddox, Andy Ray Band, Bob Jones & The Blue Ridge Mountain Boys, Cold Thunder, No Strings Attached, Sam Hill. "Band scramble" starts the festival at 11 a.m. on Saturday. All performances held outdoors. A covered area is available for the audience. Over 30 high quality art booths and over 10 food booths. Hours: Saturday 11 a.m.-9 p.m., Sunday 10 a.m.-6 p.m. Tickets: $25 for the weekend. Advance ticket sales available. A, FF, EF, VF, RF, R, MR, RR, CO, CN, S, RVO, HO, M

Contact: Joe Ross, Myrtle Creek Bluegrass Festival, P.O. Box 5094, Roseburg, OR 97470 • Phone: 503-673-9759 or 503-863-3171

Pennsylvania

7TH ANNUAL ANDALUSIA BLUEGRASS DAY
September 15
Pulaski Park, Andalusia, PA

Since 1989. Annual attendance is 200. The Andrew Barthmaier Memorial Scholarship Fund was created from donations made by the family and friends of Andrew Barthmaier, an outstanding student and aspiring musician who died tragically at the age of twelve after being struck by an automobile. Each year the fund awards a scholarship to a member of the Charles Borromeo School graduation class which Andrew attended. The fund was seeded by money Andrew's parents received from his insurance policy as a Bucks County Courier Times carrier. The bluegrass concert was set up a short time later to continue funding the scholarship. At the heart of the event is Fran Barthmaier's own band, Friends to the End, also known as the Andalusia Jug Band. Andrew played side-by-side with his father in this band until his death. Each year the event brings in an increasingly talented group of accompanying acts. This year's featured performers: Flexible Flyer and Fred Moore. Past headliners: Mountain Laurel Bluegrass Band and James Bailey. Performances held outdoors with an indoor venue in case of rain. Hours: noon to 7 p.m. Tickets: $7, children (under 12) free. Advance ticket sales available. A, FF, EF, R, MR, M

Contact: Fran Barthmaier, Annual Andalusia Bluegrass Day, 1155 Evelyn Avenue, Andalusia, PA 19020 • Phone: 215-638-9453 or 215-739-5038

A = wheelchair accessible   I = interpreter for hearing impaired   F = food   FF = fast food   EF = ethnic food
VF = vegetarian food   RF = regional food   R = restaurants nearby   P = pets welcome   CC = credit cards

7TH ANNUAL CANYON COUNTRY BLUEGRASS FESTIVAL
July 12-14
Stony Fork Creek Campgrounds, Wellsboro, PA

Since 1989. Annual attendance is 1,000. "Mountain majesty" — nestled in the Pennsylvania Grand Canyon near Pine Creek Gorge. This family-oriented event features traditional to progressive bluegrass music. Past performers: Tony Rice, Tony Trishka, Del McCoury, Lonesome River Band. All performances held outdoors. A covered area is available for the audience. Musical competitions, children's activities, and concession area. Hours: Friday 7 p.m.-11 p.m., Saturday 9 a.m.-1 a.m., Sunday 9:30 a.m.-5 p.m. Call 1-800-PA-GRASS for ticket prices and information. Advance ticket sales available. A, F, R, P (on leash; not in stage area), RR, CO, S, RVO, HO, M

Contact: Debbie Rubin or Pete Herres, Annual Canyon Country Bluegrass Festival, 2 Charles Street, Wellsboro, PA 16901 • Phone: 800-PA-GRASS (tickets) or 717-724-7572 or 717-724-4424 • Fax: 717-724-5103

9TH ANNUAL SPRING GULCH FOLK FESTIVAL
May 17-19
Spring Gulch Resort, New Holland, PA

Since 1987. Annual attendance is 4,000 to 5,000. This is a family-oriented musical festival in the quiet countryside in the heart of Amish farmlands at a premier camping resort (one of the "top 10" in the USA). The types of music featured are folk, bluegrass, country, blues, newgrass, and folk pop with nationally known artists. Past performers include Doc Watson, Tom Paxton, The Roches, Bill Miller, Beausoleil, and Robin and Linda Williams. There are musical competitions, workshops, children's activities, crafts and dancing (folk, traditional and ethnic). Performances are indoors and outdoors. Hours: Friday 8 p.m. to Sunday 5 p.m. Tickets range from $10 to $75. Advance sales available. A, FF, EF, VF, RF, R, P (on leash), CC, MR, CO, S, RVO, HO, M

Contact: Elaine Jackson, 475 Lynch Road, New Holland, PA 17557 • Phone: 800-255-5744 • Fax: 717-355-9739

16TH ANNUAL OLD FIDDLERS PICNIC
August 3
Lancaster County Central Park, Lancaster, PA

Since 1981. Annual attendance is 1,500. This is a local bluegrass festival with a truly beautiful location in a shady park next to a quiet river. It features bluegrass and old-time music. Musical competitions and square dancing. All performances held outdoors. Hours: 10 a.m.-6 p.m. Tickets are $2 per car. FF, R (2 mi.), P, MR, RR, CO, RVN, HN, M

Contact: John Gerencser, 1050 Rockford Road, Lancaster, PA 17602 • Phone: 717-299-8217 • Fax: 717-295-5942

MR = modern restrooms   RR = rustic restrooms   CO = camping on-site   CN = camping nearby   S = hot showers
RVO = RVs on-site   RVN = RVs nearby   HO = hookups on-site   HN = hookups nearby   M = motels nearby

BERLIN COMMUNITY GROVE BLUEGRASS FESTIVAL
September 1-2
Berlin Community Grove, Berlin, PA

Since 1978. This is one of the few free family festivals. Lots of camping areas in a tree-lined grove. Playground and ball field for the kids. Pets and 24-hour parking are welcome. Bring your own instruments and use the P.A. system. Plenty of parking lot picking – 24 hours. Square dancing. All performances are held outdoors. There is a covered area for the audience. Hours are 11-11 each day. The festival and camping are free. A, FF, RF, R, P, RR, RVO, M

Contact: Todd & JoAnne Dively, P.O. Box 203, Berlin, PA 15530 • Phone: 814-267-3097 or 814-445-7143

BLUE MOUNTAIN GOSPEL MUSIC FESTIVAL
August 24-September 1
Kempton Community Grounds, Kempton, PA

Since 1975. Annual attendance 8,000 to 10,000. This clean, family festival features southern and bluegrass gospel music. This year's headliners: Lewis Family, Isaacs, Doyle Lawson, and a total of 40 other groups. Children's activities. Performances held both indoors and outdoors. A covered area is available for the audience outdoors. Weekend hours are noon to midnight. Call for prices. A, FF (meals), CC, MR, CO, RVO, RVN, HO, HN, M

Contact: Richard Carper, Blue Mountain Gospel Music Festival, P.O. Box 4704, Lancaster, PA 17604 • Phone: 717-872-5615 • Fax: 717-872-5876

CIRCLE OF FRIENDS BLUEGRASS FESTIVAL
January 12-14
Days Inn, Butler, PA

Since 1993. This is a totally free music festival – no bands are paid, and no one pays to hear the music. Expenses are covered through donations only. Bluegrass music is featured with no fewer than twenty bands over the weekend. Children's activities and dancing (clogging). All performances are held indoors. Call the hotel at (412) 287-6761 to reserve rooms. Mention the Bluegrass Weekend and give the date. Cut off date for reservations is 12/12/95. A, F (meals in motel restaurant), FF (nearby restaurants), R, MR, S, M

Contact: Charlie Burton, Circle Of Friends Bluegrass Festival, 170 North Camp Run Road, Harmony, PA 16037 • Phone: 412-368-3938

A = wheelchair accessible   I = interpreter for hearing impaired   F = food   FF = fast food   EF = ethnic food
VF = vegetarian food   RF = regional food   R = restaurants nearby   P = pets welcome   CC = credit cards

GETTYSBURG BLUEGRASS FESTIVAL
May 2-5, August 22-25
Granite Hill Campground, Gettysburg, PA

Since 1979. Annual attendance is 3,000 to 4,000. Held in a beautiful setting near historic Gettysburg (easy access), this festival features great sound and performances highlighting traditional and contemporary bluegrass music and some traditional country and old-timey music. This year's headliners include: Alison Krauss, Del McCoury, Johnson Mountain Boys, Ralph Stanley, Country Gentlemen, and many more. Musical competitions, workshops, children's activities, crafts area, and clog dancing lessons. All performances held outdoors. Hours: 11 a.m.-midnight each day. Tickets range from $10 to $65. Advance ticket sales available. A, F, R, CC, MR, RR, CO, CN, S, RVO, RVN, HO, HN, M

Contact: Joe Cornett, Gettysburg Bluegrass Festival, 3340 Fairfield Road, Gettysburg, PA 17325 • Phone: 717-642-8749 or 800-642-TENT (for ticket charges only)

JERSEY TOWN BLUEGRASS FESTIVAL
July 4-7
Across from Diehl's Farm Market, Rt. 642 (Jerseytown Rd.)
Jerseytown, PA

Since 1992. Annual attendance is 300±. Tentative headliners for this year: Jim & Jesse, Osborne Brothers, Larry Sparks, Stevens Family, Lost & Found, Allen Greeden & VA Cutups, Clark Family, and many others. Crafts area. Free pig roast on July 4 from 5-6 p.m. Hours: Thursday 6-12 p.m., Friday and Saturday 11 a.m.-midnight, Sunday 11 a.m.-5:45 p.m. Tickets: weekend in advance $30, at gate $35. Thursday $10. Friday in advance $12, at gate $15. Saturday in advance $15, at gate $18. Sunday $10 in advance, $12 at gate. A (parking only), FF, EF, VF, RF, R, P (on leash), RR, CO, S, RVO, HO, M

Contact: Walt Laubach Jr., Jersey Town Bluegrass Festival, RD 9, Bloomsburg, PA 17815 • Phone: 717-437-2227 (night); 717-275-2491 (day); or 941-743-2795 (Dec.-April)

MOUNTAIN TOP FALL BLUEGRASS FESTIVAL
August 31-September 2
Mountain Top Campground, Tarentum, PA

Since 1992. Annual attendance is 500. Just 20 miles north of Pittsburgh with easy access from major highways. Excellent entertainment at affordable prices in a scenic, warm, family atmosphere. This year's headliner is The Clark Family. Past performers: IIIrd Tyme Out, James King. Workshops, crafts and dancing (clogging). All performances held outdoors. A covered area is available for the audience. Hours: Friday 6-12, Saturday 2-12, Sunday 12-6. Three-day advance camper per person $20, at gate $25. Three-day advance non-camper $30 per person. Adult tickets Friday and Sunday $10, Saturday $20. Children (under 12) free with adult. A, FF, EF, VF, R, P (on leash), RR, CO, RVO, HO, M

MR = modern restrooms   RR = rustic restrooms   CO = camping on-site   CN = camping nearby   S = hot showers
RVO = RVs on-site   RVN = RVs nearby   HO = hookups on-site   HN = hookups nearby   M = motels nearby

Contact: Ed & Francine Michaels, 522 Sun Mine Road, RD #2, Tarentum, PA 15084
• Phone: 412-224-1511

MOUNTAIN TOP SPRING BLUEGRASS FESTIVAL
May 31-June 2
Mountain Top Campground, Tarentum, PA

Since 1992. Annual attendance is 500. Just 20 miles north of Pittsburgh with easy access from major highways. Excellent entertainment at affordable prices in a scenic, warm, family atmosphere. This year's headliners: Charlie Waller, James King, Stevens Family. Past performers: IIIrd Tyme Out, James King. Workshops, crafts and dancing (clogging). All performances held outdoors. A covered area is available for the audience. Hours: Friday 6-12, Saturday 2-12, Sunday 12-6. Three-day advance camper per person $20, at gate $25. Three-day advance non-camper $30 per person. Adult tickets Friday and Sunday $10, Saturday $20. Children (under 12) free with adult. A, FF, EF, VF, R, P (on leash), RR, CO, RVO, HO, M

Contact: Ed & Francine Michaels, 522 Sun Mine Road, RD #2, Tarentum, PA 15084
• Phone: 412-224-1511

OLD BEDFORD VILLAGE BLUEGRASS FESTIVAL
July 20-21
Old Bedford Village, Bedford, PA

Since 1981. Annual attendance is 1,000 per day. The festival takes place in an 1800 reconstructed Pioneer Village. Very well organized. Alcohol free. Family oriented. Free camping (no hook-up). Easy access (1/2 mile off PA turnpike). This year's headliners: The Lewis Family plus at least six other headlining acts. Crafts area. All performances held outdoors. A covered area is available for the audience. Hours: noon to 8 p.m. Tickets prices vary depending on day and events. Discounted two-day passes available. A, FF, RF, R, P (not under tent), RR, CN, RVO, RVN, HN, M

Contact: Jamie Nesbit, Old Bedford Village Bluegrass Festival, P.O. Box 1976, Bedford, PA 15522 • Phone: 814-623-1156 or 800-238-4347 • Fax: 814-623-1158

WISE OWL MOUNTAIN JAM '96
August 8-11
Tombs Farm, Ulysses, PA

Since 1993. Annual attendance is 3,000. This is a very family-oriented event with children's workshops and band contest, pony pull, and a Civil War living history reenactment. Past performers include Ralph Stanley, Seldom Scene, Del McCoury, Lonesome River, Lou Reid, Terry Baucom, Stevens Family, U.S. Navy Band. Musical competitions, workshops, children's activities, crafts area. All performances held indoors. A covered area is available for the audience. Hours: Thursday 6-11 p.m., Friday 5 p.m.-midnight, Saturday 10 a.m.-midnight, Sunday 11 a.m.-8:30 p.m. Tickets: $30 in advance (before July 23); $32 at gate. A, F (home cooked), FF, R, P ($5 fee; on leash only), RR, CO, CN, RVO, RVN, HN, M

A = wheelchair accessible   I = interpreter for hearing impaired   F = food   FF = fast food   EF = ethnic food
VF = vegetarian food   RF = regional food   R = restaurants nearby   P = pets welcome   CC = credit cards

Contact: Dennis & Margaret Mealey, Wise Owl Mountain Jam, P.O. Box 175, Ulysses, PA 16948 • Phone: 814-435-2337

Rhode Island

17TH ANNUAL CAJUN & BLUEGRASS MUSIC FESTIVAL
August 30-September 1
Stepping Stone Ranch, Escoheag, RI

Since 1980. Annual attendance is 3,000. This festival combines two disparate styles of music – old-time / bluegrass and Cajun / Zydeco. Dance is central to Cajun and Creole cultures, and in this spirit the festival has built two large dance floors (one beneath a tent) and hosts 14 hours of nonstop dancing. Free dance lessons are given both days so that by evening you are ready to waltz, Cajun two-step, Zydeco shuffle, or just "kick up yer heels." Cajun and Creole foods, like the music, are guar-on-teed to fire up the blood and keep you dancin' all night. Traditional cultural foods such as gumbo, andouille sausage, blackened fish, boudin, etouffee, jambalaya, and red beans and rice are served along with famous New Orleans sweets. The festival is extra fun because of the participatory activities for the children. Kids of all ages can occupy themselves making costumes and jewelry for their Mardi Gras parade each day at 5 p.m. Workshops and crafts areas. Events held both indoors and outdoors. Past performers: CJ Chenier & The Red Hot Louisiana Band, Steve Riley & The Mamou Playboys, Lonesome River Band, Austin Lounge Lizards, Robin & Linda Williams, The Cox Family, Walter Mouton & The Scott Playboys, Laurie Lewis & Grant Street, The Poullard Brothers. Hours: 11 a.m.-past midnight. Call for ticket information. Advance ticket sales with discounts available. A, EF, CC, RR, CO, RVO, RVN, HN, M

Contact: Franklin Zawacki, 151 Althea Street, Providence, RI 02907 • Phone: 401-351-6312

South Carolina

27TH ANNUAL SOUTH CAROLINA STATE
BLUEGRASS FESTIVAL
November 28-30
Convention Center, Oak Street at 21st Avenue, Myrtle Beach, SC

Since 1969. Family entertainment and top bluegrass bands. Past performers: Bill Monroe, Osborne Brothers, Jim & Jesse, Lewis Family. All performances held indoors. Crafts area. Hours: noon-11 p.m. daily. Call for ticket information. Reserved seating and general admission. A, FF, R, CC, MR, CN, RVN, HN, M

MR = modern restrooms   RR = rustic restrooms   CO = camping on-site   CN = camping nearby   S = hot showers
RVO = RVs on-site   RVN = RVs nearby   HO = hookups on-site   HN = hookups nearby   M = motels nearby

Contact: Norman Adams or Tony Anderson, P.O. Box 98, 112 N. Park Street, Dahlonega, GA 30533 • Phone: 706-864-7203 • Fax: 706-864-1037

South Dakota

BLACK HILLS BLUEGRASS FESTIVAL
June 28-30
Mystery Mountain Resort, Rapid City, SD

Since 1981. Annual attendance is 650. The festival is celebrating its new home with a beautiful new amphitheater nestled in the trees of the Black Hills. It is a small festival with an atmosphere of a family reunion where people come to meet old friends and make new ones and share music with each other in jam sessions after the concerts. Features bluegrass and acoustic music. This year's headliners: The Chapman Family. Others to be announced. Past performers: Berline, Crary & Hickman, Norman Blake, Doug Dillard Band, John Hartford, Bryan Bowers, John McCutcheon, Mike Cross, Blue Highway. All performances held outdoors. Workshops and dancing (clogging). Hours: Friday 7 p.m.-10:30 p.m., Saturday 9 a.m.-10:30 p.m., Sunday 10 a.m.-noon. Tickets: single show $10; all day Saturday $16; weekend $22; children under 12 free. Advance ticket discount $1 single show, $2 discount others. Sunday gospel show free – with offering. A, F (picnic dinner on Saturday evening), FF, R, RR, CO, S, RVO, HO, M (on site)

Contact: Carol McConnell, Black Hills Bluegrass Festival, 713 Seventh Street, Rapid City, SD 57701 • Phone: 605-394-4101 • Fax: 605-394-6121

Tennessee

ANNUAL APPALACHIAN DUMPLIN' FESTIVAL
September (call for exact date)
Winfield City Hall, Winfield, TN

Since 1985. Annual attendance is 4,000 to 5,000. Home-town hospitality, dumplings (all varieties), and great bluegrass and gospel music make this festival truly special. Musical competitions, children's activities, crafts area, and line dancing. All performances held outdoors. Hours: Saturday 10 a.m.-10 p.m., Sunday 1 p.m.-6 p.m. Admission is FREE. A, FF, RF, R, MR, RVN, HN, M

Contact: Robyn McBroom, Annual Appalachian Dumplin' Festival, P.O. Box 38, Winfield, TN 37892 • Phone: 615-569-6139 • Fax: 615-615-2569

BELL WITCH BLUEGRASS COMPETITION
August 9-10
Old Bell School Grounds, Adams, TN

Since 1945. Annual attendance is 400. Held in a beautiful outdoor setting under a covered area. A chance for bluegrass enthusiasts to meet, fraternize and "do their thing" before an enthusiastic audience. The festival is sponsored by the Adams Community Men's Club. Musical competitions, children's activities, crafts area, and dancing (clogging, team square dancing). All performances held outdoors. Music begins Friday 7 p.m. and Saturday 10 a.m. Tickets: Friday $3, Saturday $4, includes competition entry. Children (under 12) $1. A, RF, R (14 mi.), P, RR, RVO, HO, M (14 mi.)

Contact: Terry Carroll or Omer Gene Brooksher or Fred Goodman, Bell Witch Bluegrass Competition, P.O. Box 28, Adams, TN 37010 • Phone: 615-228-7095 or 615-696-2589 or 615-696-2469

COKE OVENS BLUEGRASS FESTIVAL
May 31-June 1
Coke Ovens Park, Dunlap, TN

Since 1987. Annual attendance is 1,500 to 2,000. A smooth, well-run bluegrass competition in the heart of the Sequatchie Valley area of Tennessee at one of the best park facilities in the South. Includes band competitions, banjo, guitar, fiddle, mandolin, harmonica, and junior musicians. Past performers: Dismembered Tennesseans, Charlie Lourin, Foster Family, Fritts Family, and many other regional performers. Crafts area. Clogging competition. Performances held outdoors. A covered area is available for the audience. Hours: Friday 7 p.m. until ??; Saturday 10 a.m.-10 p.m. Tentative prices: Friday $2 donation; Saturday $4 donation. A, FF, R, P (under strict control), MR, CO, RVO, RVN, HO (limited), HN, M (1 local)

Contact: Edward R. Brown, 65 Lockhart Road, Dunlap, TN 37327 • Phone: 423-949-2294 or 423-949-3060

COUSIN JAKE MEMORIAL BLUEGRASS FESTIVAL
March 8-9
Historic Gem Theater, Etowah, TN

Since 1995. Annual attendance is 600+. The festival is held in memory of "Cousin" Jake Tullock. Jake was a local Etowah boy who spent more than 25 years as a professional bluegrass musician. Most of his career was as bass player for Flatt & Scruggs. This year's headliners: Josh Graves, Steve Kaufman, Hiwassee Ridge. Musical competitions and workshops. All performances held indoors. Hours: Friday 6-11 p.m., Saturday 10 a.m.-11 p.m. Tickets: Friday $7, Saturday $8, children $4. Advance ticket sales available. A, FF, RF, R, MR, CN, RVO, RVN, HN, M

Contact: Charles Munn, Etowah Arts Commission, Cousin Jake Memorial Bluegrass Festival, P.O. Box 193, Etowah, TN 37331 • Phone: 615-263-7608

MR = modern restrooms   RR = rustic restrooms   CO = camping on-site   CN = camping nearby   S = hot showers
RVO = RVs on-site   RVN = RVs nearby   HO = hookups on-site   HN = hookups nearby   M = motels nearby

FROG BOTTOM BLUEGRASS FESTIVAL
August 3-4
Frog Bottom, Cornersville, TN

Since 1982. Annual attendance is 3,000. A family event which includes musical competitions, children's activities and competitions, crafts and buck dancing. Past performers: Bill Monroe, Osborne Brothers, Kitty Wells. All performances are held outdoors. Catfish supper 5-7 on Saturday. Hours are 6 p.m.-10 p.m. on Saturday, and starting at 9 a.m. on Sunday. Tickets are $3 for Friday, $5 for Saturday. Children (12 and under) free with adult admission. A, FF, RF, R, P, MR, CO, RVN, HN, M

Contact: Lawrence Haynes, P.O. Box 91, Cornersville, TN 37047 • Phone: 615-293-2626

MUSEUM OF APPALACHIA'S TENNESSEE FALL HOMECOMING
October 10-13
Museum of Appalachia, Norris, TN

Since 1979. Attendance is 50,000+. With a gathering of over 400 old-time Southern Appalachian musicians and singers, and genuine mountain craftsmen and artisans, the Museum of Appalachia's annual Tennessee Fall Homecoming is reminiscent of an old-time mountain homecoming. Demonstrations include such rural and pioneer activities as rail splitting, molasses boiling, wool spinning, saw milling and sheep herding. Over 250 locally and nationally known musicians perform simultaneously on 4 "stages" while regional authors autograph their books and local cooks serve traditional Southern food such as pinto beans, cornbread and fried pies. Participants and visitors return each year to celebrate and commemorate the heritage and culture of Southern Appalachia. Past performers: Bill Monroe, Grandpa Jones, John Hartford, Mac Wiseman, Raymond Fairchild, Janette and Joe Carter, George Thacker, and some 200 more. Headliners anticipated for this year: John Hartford, Mac Wiseman, Grandpa Jones, Bill Monroe, Roy Acuff's Smoky Mountain Boys, Raymond Fairchild, Mike Seeger. Crafts, clogging and buck dancing. All performances held outdoors. Hours: 9 a.m. until dusk. Call for current ticket prices. Discounts given for tickets purchased before 9/24. A (limited), FF, RF, R, CC, RR, CN, RVN, HN, M

Contact: John Rice Irwin, Director, Box 0318, Norris, TN 37828 • Phone: 423-494-7680 or 423-494-0514 • Fax: 423-494-8957

NINE MILE VOLUNTEER FIRE CO. BLUEGRASS FESTIVAL
May 10-11, September 20-21
Nine Mile Fire Department, Pikeville, TN

Annual attendance is 3,000. Features bluegrass and gospel music and good, clean family fun and entertainment. Held rain or shine. Crafts area. Buck dancing. All performances held outdoors. A sheltered area is available for the audience. Hours: Friday 7 p.m. to midnight (?), Saturday noon until ??. Tickets: Friday night $2, Saturday $4, 2-day ticket $5. Children under 12 admitted free. A, FF, RF, R (10 mi.), MR, CO, S, M (10 mi.)

A = wheelchair accessible   I = interpreter for hearing impaired   F = food   FF = fast food   EF = ethnic food
VF = vegetarian food   RF = regional food   R = restaurants nearby   P = pets welcome   CC = credit cards

Contact: Louis W. Edmons or Gary Edmons, Bluegrass Festival, Rt. 1, Box 126B, Pikeville, TN 37367 • Phone: 615-533-2455 or 615-533-2720

NINE MILE-EDMONS FAMILY BLUEGRASS FESTIVAL
June 21-22, August 2-3
The Edmons Farm – Nine Mile, Pikeville, TN

Annual attendance is 2,000 to 3,000. Features bluegrass and gospel music and good, clean family fun and entertainment. Held rain or shine. Crafts area. Buck dancing. All performances held outdoors. A sheltered area is available for the audience. Hours: Friday 7 p.m. to midnight (?), Saturday noon until ??. Tickets: Friday night $2, Saturday $4, 2-day ticket $5. Children under 12 admitted free. A, FF, RF, R (10 mi.), MR, CO, S, M (10 mi.)

Contact: Louis W. Edmons, Edmons Family Bluegrass Festival, Rt. 1, Box 126B, Pikeville, TN 37367 • Phone: 615-533-2455 or 615-533-2720

SMITHVILLE FIDDLERS JAMBOREE & CRAFTS FESTIVAL
July 5-6
On the Square, Downtown, Smithville, TN

Since 1971. Annual attendance is 75,000 to 90,000. Features old-time, bluegrass and gospel music. The event preserves the old-time, Appalachian type music and dance. All performers are "amateurs." Includes competitions, crafts, buck dancing and clogging. All performances are held outdoors. Friday hours: 10 a.m.-midnight. Saturday: 9 a.m.-midnight. Admission is free. A, FF, R, P, RR, CN, RVN, HN, M

Contact: Darlene Willingham, Wanda Johannsen (crafts), Fiddlers Jamboree, P.O. Box 64, Smithville, TN 37166 • Phone: 615-597-4163 or 615-597-5024 (for crafts)

SMOKY MOUNTAIN FIDDLERS CONVENTION
August 23-24
Legion Field, Loudon, TN

Since 1982. Annual attendance 5,000+. The Smoky Mountain Fiddlers Convention is an annual bluegrass competition with over $5,000 awarded in prize money. Children's activities, crafts and dancing (buck dancing and clogging). The event is held outdoors under a tent and grandstand. Hours are Friday 6 p.m.-midnight; Saturday 10 a.m.-midnight. Tickets are $5/day per person. Children under 12 are free. Advance ticket sales available. A, FF, R, MR, RR, CO, CN, RVO, RVN, HN, M

Contact: Dr. Michael E. Bowman, 800 Mulberry Street, Loudon, TN 37774 • Phone: 615-458-4352 • Fax: 615-458-2845

MR = modern restrooms   RR = rustic restrooms   CO = camping on-site   CN = camping nearby   S = hot showers
RVO = RVs on-site   RVN = RVs nearby   HO = hookups on-site   HN = hookups nearby   M = motels nearby

SMOKY MOUNTAIN GOSPEL SINGING
September 20-22
Sevier County Fairgrounds, Sevierville, TN

Since 1989. Annual attendance is 1,000+. Free to the public, this festival is nestled in the beautiful foothills of the Smokies. It offers some of the finest gospel music around – bluegrass gospel, Southern gospel and country gospel – and features local artists as well as groups from other areas and states. Performances are held both indoors and outdoors. A covered area is available for the audience outdoors. Hours: 7 p.m.-10:30 p.m. Friday and Saturday, with variable hours on Sunday. Admission is free (donations accepted). A, FF, R, MR, CO, RVN, HN, M

Contact: Don Howell, 2140 Chapman Highway, Sevierville, TN 37876 • Phone: 615-453-2620 • Fax: 615-428-1625 / Attn. Don Howell

THE VIC RHODES TRADITIONAL MUSIC FESTIVAL
May 24-25
Crawford Airport, 6 mi. S. of Somerville off I-40, Williston, TN

Since 1994. Annual attendance is 1,000±. Hundreds of acres of beautiful, neatly manicured grounds. Plenty of parking and free camping. Lots of great food and super bluegrass and old time music. Over $2,500 in prize money. Not restricted to play with just one band. This is a jammin' festival. Buck dancing competition. All events held outdoors. A covered area is available for the audience. Hours: 4 p.m.-?? on Friday; 1 p.m.-?? on Saturday. Price: $5/day, $10/weekend. Includes competition entry fee. No charge to enter contests. Advance tickets available. A, FF, R, P, RR, CO, RVO, M

Contact: Jeff Long or Sarge McCann, 106 Radio Road, Jackson, TN 38301 • Phone: 901-422-5315 or 901-422-5906

Texas

20TH ANNUAL SALMON LAKE PARK BLUEGRASS FESTIVAL
August 30-September 1
Salmon Lake Park, Grapeland, TX

Since 1976. Annual attendance 3,000. Great bluegrass bands and old-fashioned hospitality. Past performers: Larry Sparks, The Cox Family, Warrior Rivers Boys, Tennessee Gentlemen, Bluegrass Tradition. Children's activities and crafts area. All performances held outdoors. Hours: Friday 7-11:30 p.m., Saturday 10 a.m.-midnight, Sunday 10 a.m.-5:30 p.m. Three-day ticket is $20. A, FF, R, P, MR, CO, CN, S, RVO, RVN, HO, HN, M

Contact: Fannie Salmon or Joe Featherston, P.O. Box 483, Grapeland, TX 75844 • Phone: 409-687-2594 or 903-849-2211

A = wheelchair accessible I = interpreter for hearing impaired F = food FF = fast food EF = ethnic food
VF = vegetarian food RF = regional food R = restaurants nearby P = pets welcome CC = credit cards

Bluegrass Jamboree

May 23-26
Oakdale Park, Glen Rose, TX

Since 1972. Annual attendance is 3,000±. Features bluegrass music with continual jam sessions all over the park, day and night. Children's activities and crafts area. All performances held outdoors. Hours: 1 p.m.-midnight. Tentative pricing $10 per day per person. Advance ticket sales available. A, FF, R, P, CC, MR, CN, S, RVO, RVN, HO, HN, M

Contact: Pete & Whimp May or Scott & Judy May, Bluegrass Jamboree, P.O. Box 548, Glen Rose, TX 76043 • Phone: 817-897-2321

Bluegrass Reunion

October 4-6
Oakdale Park, Glen Rose, TX

Since 1972. Annual attendance is 3,000±. Features bluegrass music with continual jam sessions all over the park, day and night. Children's activities and crafts area. All performances held outdoors. Hours: 1 p.m.-midnight. Tentative pricing $10 per day per person. Advance ticket sales available. A, FF, R, P, CC, MR, CN, S, RVO, RVN, HO, HN, M

Contact: Pete & Whimp May or Scott & Judy May, Bluegrass Reunion, P.O. Box 548, Glen Rose, TX 76043 • Phone: 817-897-2321

Boo Grass Picking Around the Campfire

October 22-26
Strange Family Bluegrass RV Park, Texarkana, TX

Since 1983. Annual attendance is 500. This is a bluegrass Halloween party. Friendly atmosphere, food, lots of jamming, workshops and craft activities. Performances held both indoors and outdoors. Jamming, crafts and fellowship are ongoing throughout the week. A Halloween party on Saturday evening. No admission charge, only for camping. ($7 for full hook-ups; $5 for electric and water). A, F (pot luck or covered dish supper), R, P (on leash), MR, S, RVO, RVN, HO, HN, M

Contact: Sam or Sharon Strange, Boo Grass Picking Around the Campfire, Rt. 2, Box 327-B2, Texarkana, TX 75501 • Phone: 903-792-9018 (evening) or 903-838-0361 (day)

Central Texas Bluegrass Association's Spring Music Festival

May 12
Zilker Park, Austin, TX

Since 1987. Annual attendance is 1,000. Held in a beautiful hillside setting, this festival features bluegrass and related musical styles (Irish, old-time), great jamming, and

---

MR = modern restrooms   RR = rustic restrooms   CO = camping on-site   CN = camping nearby   S = hot showers
RVO = RVs on-site   RVN = RVs nearby   HO = hookups on-site   HN = hookups nearby   M = motels nearby

14 bands in one day! Workshops, children's activities and crafts vary from year to year. All performances held outdoors under plentiful shade trees. Past performers: Austin Lounge Lizards, The Bad Livers, Leon Valley Bluegrass, TVA, Jim O'Brien. Hours: 10-8. Admission is free. FF, VF, R, MR, M

Contact: Eddie Collins, 8407 Loralinda Drive, Austin, TX 78753-5844 • Phone: 512-836-8255 • Fax: 512-346-2599

Eagle Mountain Bluegrass & Old Tyme Country Music Festival
September 27-29
Red Sox Ball Park, Van Horn, TX

Since 1989. This festival has doubled in size each year since it began. Features bluegrass and old tyme country music and plenty of campfire jammin'. Ten to twelve bands, plus third annual bar-b-cue beef cookoff, and Eagle Mountain Comedy Gunfight Show. Workshops, children's activities and crafts. All performances held outdoors. No food served, but there are eight cafes within three blocks. Friday: 7 p.m.-1 a.m., Saturday noon-1 a.m., Sunday 10 a.m.-??. Tickets: $5 Friday, $7 Saturday, $10 weekend package. Advance ticket sales available. A, R, P (on leash), MR, CO, CN, RVO, RVN, HO, HN, M

Contact: Dale & Lou Evans, Eagle Mountain BG Festival, Box 595, Van Horn, TX 79855 • Phone: 915-283-2564

Picking Around The Campfire
March 26-30, April 23-27, September 24-28
Strange Family Park, Texarkana, TX

Since 1983. Annual attendance is 500. Friendly, family-oriented festival held in a beautiful park. Good jam sessions. Past performers: Country Gentlemen, Karl Shiflett & Big Country, Liberty Bluegrass, New Crop of Grass. Workshops and crafts area. Performances held both indoors and outdoors. Music runs all day and through the night. The only charge is for camping ($5 per day with water and electric; $7 per day for full hook-ups). A, F (pot luck or covered dish supper), R, P (on leash), S, MR, RVO, RVN, HO, HN, M

Contact: Sam or Sharon Strange, Picking Around The Campfire, Rt. 2, Box 327-B2, Texarkana, TX 75501 • Phone: 903-792-9018 (evening) or 903-838-0361 (day)

Plum Creek Park Bluegrass Festival
April 18-20, September 26-28
Plum Creek Bluegrass Music Park, Exit 189 off I-45, Dew, TX

Since 1985. Annual attendance is 1,200. Great family entertainment. Past performers: Karl Shiflett & Big Country, The Chapman Family, Bill Jones & The Bluegrass Travelers, Bill & Laurie Sky, Ft. English Express, Gary Brewer and the Kentucky Ramblers. Clogging exhibition on Saturday. Workshops and crafts area. All performances held

---

A = wheelchair accessible   I = interpreter for hearing impaired   F = food   FF = fast food   EF = ethnic food
VF = vegetarian food   RF = regional food   R = restaurants nearby   P = pets welcome   CC = credit cards

outdoors. A covered area is available for the audience. Hours: Thursday 6 p.m.–11 p.m., Friday and Saturday 10 a.m.–11 p.m. Thursday $7, Friday $9, Saturday $10. A three-day pass is $22. Electrical hookups $7 daily. A, FF, R, P (on leash), RR, CO, S, RVO, RVN, HO, HN, M

Contact: Karl Shiflett, P.O. Box 576, Groesbeck, TX 76642 • Phone: 817-729-3702 or 903-389-6249

Rib Rustlers Bluegrass Campout
March 15-17
Laurence E. Wood Park on Hwy. 118, Ft. Davis, TX

Since 1994. There is no stage show at this event – just jamming, camping and BBQing. Held high up in the Davis Mountains where it is cool among the pines. This is mostly a musicians' jam session with bands from Texas and New Mexico, but the public is welcome. Admission is free. F (pot luck by everyone on Saturday), P, RR, CO, CN, RVO, RVN

Contact: Dale & Lou Evans, Rib Rustlers Bluegrass Campout, Box 595, Van Horn, TX 79855 • Phone: 915-283-2564

Second Annual Lone Wolf Bluegrass Festival
May 24-26
Ruddick Park, Colorado City, TX

Since 1995. The festival was named in recognition of Chief Lone Wolf, A Kiowa tribal leader living in this area during the mid-1800's. The festival is nestled beneath shade trees along the banks of Lone Wolf Creek in the city's beautiful Ruddick Park. Past performers: Roy Thackerson "The Fingerless Fiddler," plus other great bluegrass bands. Musical competitions, children's activities, and crafts area. All performances held outdoors. Hours: Friday noon-11 p.m., Saturday 7:30 a.m.-midnight, Sunday 8 a.m.-noon. Tickets: $5 Friday and Sunday, $8 Saturday, $15 weekend pass, children (12 and under) free. Advance ticket sales available. A, F, R, MR, RR, CO, CN, RVO, RVN, HO, HN, M

Contact: Doris Shutt, EVP, Lone Wolf Bluegrass Festival, P.O. Box 242, 157 W. Second Street, Colorado City, TX 79512 • Phone: 915-728-3403 • Fax: 915-728-2911

Southeast Texas Bluegrass Music Association Jam & Show
Third Saturday monthly:
January 20, February 17, March 16, April 20, May 18, June 15, July 20, August 17, September 21, October 19, November 16, December 21
Elementary School, Sour Lake, TX

Since 1976. Annual attendance is 250 to 300. Features bluegrass and fiddling. All performances indoors. Hours are 6 p.m.-11 p.m. Admission is free. A, F, R, MR, RVN, HN, M (20 miles)

MR = modern restrooms	RR = rustic restrooms	CO = camping on-site	CN = camping nearby	S = hot showers
RVO = RVs on-site	RVN = RVs nearby	HO = hookups on-site	HN = hookups nearby	M = motels nearby

Contact: Edy Mathews, 7110 Lewis Drive, Beaumont, TX 77708-1017 • Phone: 409-892-5767

SPRING CREEK BLUEGRASS CLUB FESTIVAL
October 25-27
Coushatte Recreation Ranch, Bellville, TX

Annual attendance is 1,000. Showcases bluegrass music on a beautiful stage in a clean, family environment surrounded by large oak shade trees. Past headliners: Lewis Family, Larry Stephenson, Sand Mountain Boys, IIIrd Tyme Out. Crafts area. All performances held outdoors in good weather. An air conditioned/heated building is available if needed. Friday 7 p.m.-11 p.m. Saturday 10 a.m.-11 p.m. Sunday 10 a.m.-noon. Tickets: Friday $7, Saturday $10, Sunday $4. Three-day advance tickets (prior to October 15) $18, at gate $20. A, FF, RF, R, P (not in concert or vending areas), MR, CO, S, RVO, HO, M

Contact: Carolyn or Buddy Brockett, 9410 Dundalk, Spring, TX 77379 • Phone: 713-379-2959 or 409-865-3633 (during festival)

STRANGE FAMILY FALL BLUEGRASS FESTIVAL
August 29-September 1
Strange Family Bluegrass / RV Park, Texarkana, TX

Since 1983. Annual attendance is 3,000. Friendly, family-oriented festival held in a beautiful park. Features bluegrass and gospel music. Past performers: Tennessee Gentlemen, Lewis Family, Country Gentlemen, Mike Snyder, Bluegrass Cardinals. Workshops, children's activities, crafts area, and clogging. All performances held outdoors. A covered area is available for the audience. Hours: 10 a.m. to midnight each day. Tickets: $25 for 4-day pass plus camping fee. Advance ticket sales available. A, FF, VF, R, P (on leash; not in seating area), MR, S, RVO, RVN, HO, HN, M

Contact: Sam or Sharon Strange, Fall Bluegrass Festival, Rt. 2, Box 327-B2, Texarkana TX 75501 • Phone: 903-792-9018 (evening) or 903-838-0361 (day)

STRANGE FAMILY SPRING BLUEGRASS FESTIVAL
May 23-26
Strange Family Bluegrass / RV Park, Texarkana, TX

Since 1983. Annual attendance is 3,000 to 4,000. Friendly, family-oriented festival held in a beautiful park. Features bluegrass and gospel music. This year's headliners: Continental Divide, Drive Tyme, Blue Stem, High Standard, Goldwing Express. Past performers: Tennessee Gentlemen, Lewis Family, Country Gentlemen, Mike Snyder, Bluegrass Cardinals. Workshops, children's activities, crafts area, and clogging. All performances held outdoors. A covered area is available for the audience. Hours: 10 a.m. to midnight each day. Tickets: $25 for 4-day pass plus camping fee. Advance ticket sales available. A, FF, VF, R, P (on leash; not in seating area), MR, S, RVO, RVN, HO, HN, M

A = wheelchair accessible   I = interpreter for hearing impaired   F = food   FF = fast food   EF = ethnic food
VF = vegetarian food   RF = regional food   R = restaurants nearby   P = pets welcome   CC = credit cards

Contact: Sam or Sharon Strange, Spring Bluegrass Festival, Rt. 2, Box 327-B2, Texarkana, TX 75501 • Phone: 903-792-9018 (evening) or 903-838-0361 (day)

TRES RIOS 12TH ANNUAL FALL BLUEGRASS FESTIVAL
September 12-15
Tres Rios RV Park & Campgrounds, Glen Rose, TX

Since 1984. Annual attendance 5,000 to 6,000. Situated on 55 acres of prime Texas land, the festival boasts seven Jam'n Buildings, 40 motel rooms/cabins, 500 RV hookups, three rivers that come together, trees, smiling faces, good food, good friends and great bluegrass music. This year's headliners include David Parmley & Scott Vestal & Continental Divide, Bluegrass Cardinals, LeRoy Troy, Sand Mountain Boys, Marksmen, and Goldwing Express. Past performers include Front Range, Warrior River, Cox Family, Lauri Lewis, Chubby Wise, and The New Tradition. There are workshops and crafts. Performances are held outdoors. There is a covered area for the audience. Hours are 11-11 (may vary). A four-day pass is $30, a three-day pass is $25. Thursday, Friday and Saturday ticket prices are $10 per day. Sunday is $8. Advance ticket sales are available. A, FF, R, CC, P (not in seating area), MR, RR, S, RVO, HO, M

Contact: Linda Greshaw, P.O. Box 2112, Glen Rose, TX 76043 • Phone: 817-897-4253 • Fax: 817-897-7396

TRES RIOS 12TH ANNUAL SPRING BLUEGRASS FESTIVAL
April 25-28
Tres Rios RV Park & Campgrounds, Glen Rose, TX

Since 1984. Annual attendance is 5,000 to 6,000. Situated on 55 acres of prime Texas land, the festival boasts seven Jam'n Buildings, 40 motel rooms/cabins, 500 RV hookups, three rivers that come together, trees, smiling faces, good food, good friends and great bluegrass music. This year's headliners include David Parmley & Scott Vestal & Continental Divide, Bluegrass Cardinals, LeRoy Troy, Sand Mountain Boys, Marksmen, and Goldwing Express. Past performers include Front Range, Warrior River, Cox Family, Lauri Lewis, Chubby Wise, and The New Tradition. There are workshops and crafts. Performances are held outdoors. There is a covered area for the audience. Hours are 11-11 (may vary). A four-day pass is $30, a three-day pass is $25. Thursday, Friday and Saturday ticket prices are $10 per day. Sunday is $8. Advance ticket sales are available. A, FF, R, CC, P (not in seating area), MR, RR, S, RVO, HO, M

Contact: Linda Greshaw, P.O. Box 2112, Glen Rose, TX 76043 • Phone: 817-897-4253 • Fax: 817-897-7396

MR = modern restrooms   RR = rustic restrooms   CO = camping on-site   CN = camping nearby   S = hot showers
RVO = RVs on-site   RVN = RVs nearby   HO = hookups on-site   HN = hookups nearby   M = motels nearby

Utah

FOUNDERS TITLE COMPANY FOLK & BLUEGRASS FESTIVAL
August 11
Snow Park Lodge in Deer Valley, Park City, UT

Since 1989. Annual attendance is 1,500 to 2,000. Features acoustic folk and bluegrass music in a mountain ski area setting. Past performers include Allison Krauss & Union Station, California, Laurie Lewis, Vassar Clements, Peter Rowan. Workshops and children's activities. All performances held outdoors. Gate opens at 9:30 a.m. Acts start at 10 a.m. Prices for single tickets are $16 in advance, $18 at the gate. Family prices are $32 in advance, $35 at the gate. Seniors (62+) are $10. A, F (restaurant in lodge), R, CC, MR, CN, RVN, HN, M

Contact: Tony Polychronis, P.O. Box 2187, Salt Lake City, UT 84110 • Phone: 800-453-1360 or 801-468-7664

Vermont

BASIN BLUEGRASS FESTIVAL
July 12-14
Wymans Ponds, Brandon, VT

Since 1995. Annual attendance is 1,000. This is the only weekend bluegrass festival in Vermont. It is held in a beautiful mountain area with fields and ponds. Crafts area. All performances held outdoors. A covered area is available for the audience. Past headliners: Blistered Fingers, Larkin Family. Hours: Friday 4 p.m.-11 p.m., Saturday 10 a.m.-11 p.m., Sunday 10 a.m.-5 p.m. Ticket prices: $28 weekend pass at gate; $22.50 weekend pass in advance (by July 1, 1996). Day tickets will be available. A, FF (breakfast), R, P, MR, RR, RVO, RVN, HN, M

Contact: Linda Berry or Donna Wyman, P.O. Box 321, Brandon, VT 05733 • Phone: 802-247-3275 (Linda) or 802-247-6738 (Donna)

Virginia

4TH ANNUAL NORTHERN NECK BLUEGRASS FESTIVAL
May 25-26
Heritage Park Resort, Warsaw, VA

Since 1993. Annual attendance 500+. This festival offers bluegrass and gospel bluegrass in a scenic setting of tall pines, rolling hills and water views. Beautifully maintained grounds with clean bathrooms, hot showers, laundromat, tennis courts, Olympic swimming pool and groves. Features up and coming bluegrass bands who put their heart into the performances. This year's headliner is New Dominion Bluegrass. Past artists include Heritage, Country Current, and Southern Transfer. Musical competitions, children's activities, crafts and traditional dancing. All activities are held outdoors with a shaded area for the audience. Hours: Saturday noon-11 p.m., Sunday noon-7 p.m. Price: Two-day tickets $25-$40. Advance sales available. A, FF, RF, R, P (on leash), CC, MR, CO, CN, S, RVO, RVN, HO, HN, M

Contact: Ray Petrie, 2570 Newland Road, Warsaw, VA 22572 • Phone: 804-333-4038 • Fax: same (call first)

13TH ANNUAL MINERAL BLUEGRASS FESTIVAL
July 18-20
Walton Park, Mineral, VA

Since 1983. Family entertainment and top bluegrass bands. Past performers: Bill Monroe, Osborne Brothers, Jim & Jesse, Lewis Family. All performances held outdoors. A covered area is available for the audience. Crafts area. Hours: noon-11 p.m. daily. Call for ticket information. Advance ticket sales available. A, FF, R, CC, RR, CO, RVO, RVN, HN, M

Contact: Norman Adams or Tony Anderson, P.O. Box 98, 112 N. Park Street, Dahlonega, GA 30533 • Phone: 706-864-7203 • Fax: 706-864-1037

CARTER FAMILY MEMORIAL MUSIC FESTIVAL
August 2-3
Carter Music Center, Hiltons, VA

Since 1974. Annual attendance is 1,500 to 2,000 daily. The Carter Festival is held annually to commemorate the first country music recordings of the Carter Family and Jimmie Rodgers in August 1927. The festival is held in memory of the Carters and their musical contributions. It is an orderly, family-oriented festival. No alcoholic beverages allowed. All music is traditional old time played on acoustic instruments only. Crafts area and traditional dancing (clogging). All performances held indoors. Past headliners: Mac Wiseman, Ralph Stanley, Doc Watson, Larry Sparks, Carter Family, John Hartford, Grandpa Jones. Hours: 2-11 p.m. daily. Crafts on display all

---

MR = modern restrooms   RR = rustic restrooms   CO = camping on-site   CN = camping nearby   S = hot showers
RVO = RVs on-site   RVN = RVs nearby   HO = hookups on-site   HN = hookups nearby   M = motels nearby

day both days. Tickets: $10 per day for adults or $18 for two days, children 6-12 $1, children under 6 free. A, FF, RF, P (on leash), MR, CO, CN, RVO, RVN, M

Contact: Janette Carter, P.O. Box 111, Hiltons, VA 24258 • Phone: 703-386-9480 or 703-386-6054 (recorded message)

CENTRAL VIRGINIA FAMILY BLUEGRASS MUSIC FESTIVAL
May 16-18, August 15-17
Amelia Family Campground, Amelia, VA

Since 1980. This is a family-oriented bluegrass music festival held in a clean campground. Nothing fancy – just friendly, down-home folk. No display of alcohol permitted, and no pets in concert area. Past performers include Larry Sparks, Ric-O-Chet, Wildwood Girl, Traditional Grass. Children's activities, crafts, and traditional dancing. All performances held outdoors. A covered area is available for the audience. Hours are Thursday 6 p.m.-midnight, Friday 2 p.m.-midnight, Saturday 10 a.m.-midnight. Advance weekend tickets for Thursday through Saturday are $25. A, FF, R, MR, RR, S, RVO, RVN, HO, HN, M

Contact: John & Ferne Hutchinson, 9650 Military Road, Amelia, VA 23002 • Phone: 804-561-3011

CHRISTOPHER RUN BLUEGRASS FESTIVAL
June 13-15
Christopher Run Campground, 8 mi. N. of Mineral on 522, Mineral, VA

Since 1992. Annual attendance is 1,000 to 1,500. This festival features bluegrass and old-time music. The stage is set right on the shores of Lake Anna, overlooking the beautiful 13,600 acre lake. There is a full-service campground and a large store stacked with everything you may need. This year's headliners: The Lewis Family, Jim & Jessie, Doyle Lawson & Quicksilver, The Appalachian Trail, Bass Mountain Boys. Past performers: The Country Gentlemen, The Lewis Family, III Tyme Out, Boys From Indiana, Larry Sparks, Lost & Found. All performances held outdoors. A tent is available for the audience. Hours: Thursday 5 p.m.-midnight, Friday and Saturday noon to midnight. Advance ticket sales available. Call for prices. A, FF, R, CC, MR, S, RVO, HO, M

Contact: Jean Bazzanella, Christopher Run Bluegrass Festival, Rt. 1, Box 326, Mineral, VA 23117 • Phone: 703-894-4772 or 703-894-4744 • Fax: 703-894-4827

GRAND CAVERNS 11TH ANNUAL BLUEGRASS FESTIVAL
September 6-7
Grand Caverns Regional Park, Grottoes, VA

This festival features bluegrass music and bluegrass gospel in a beautiful park in the heart of the Shenandoah Valley. Past performers: The Lewis Family, The Country Gentlemen, The Cox Family, Mac Wiseman, The Lynn Morris Band, Jim & Jesse. Children's activities and crafts area. All performances held outdoors. Hours: Friday

---

6 p.m.-midnight; Saturday 3 p.m.-midnight. Call for ticket prices. Advance ticket sales available. A, FF, R, P, MR, RR, CO, CN, RVO, RVN, HN, M

Contact: Craig Johnson, P.O. Box 478, Grottoes, VA 24441 • Phone: 540-249-5705

GRAVES MOUNTAIN FESTIVAL OF MUSIC
May 30-June 1
Graves Mountain Lodge, Syria, VA

Since 1993. Annual attendance is 2,500. Beautiful location by a stream in the valley of the mountains. This year's headliners include Country Gentlemen, Laurie Lewis & The Grant Street Band, Mac Wiseman with Bill Emerson, Cox Family, IIIrd Tyme Out, Ralph Stanley, Larry Sparks, The New Coon Creek Girls, Tony Rice, The Whites & Jerry Douglas, The Dry Branch Fire Squad, and more. All performances held outdoors. A covered area is available for the audience. All-day barbecues, trout dinner on Friday, steak dinner on Saturday. Swimming pool and horseback riding. Advance three-day tickets $39, at the gate $55. Thursday only $12, Friday only $16, Saturday only $22. A, FF, RF (full dinners), R, CC, RR, CO, S, RVN, HN, M

Contact: Jim Graves, Graves Mountain Lodge, Inc., Route 670, Syria, VA 22743 • Phone: 540-923-4231 • Fax: 540-923-4312

GRAYSON COUNTY OLD-TIME AND BLUEGRASS FIDDLERS CONVENTION
June 28-29
Elk Creek Ball Park, Elk Creek, VA

Since 1966. Annual attendance is 4,000 to 5,000. This festival features old-time and bluegrass music in a friendly atmosphere in a very quiet rural setting. There's plenty of camping room and a fenced playground for children. Musical competitions, children's activities, crafts and dancing (flat foot and clogging). All performances are held outdoors. Hours are 5:00 p.m. until ??. Prices: Friday $5, Saturday $6, two-day ticket $10. FF, R, RR, CO, CN, M

Contact: Jerry Testerman, Route 1, Box 145-B2, Elk Creek, VA 24326 • Phone: 703-655-4740 (h) or 703-773-2822 (w)

HIGHLAND BLUEGRASS FESTIVAL
May 24-25
Highland County Fairgrounds, Monterey, VA

Since 1994. Annual attendance is 400 to 600. This festival is held in a beautiful country mountain setting with the highest mean elevation east of the Mississippi and the lowest population density. All proceeds benefit WVLS, Highland County's volunteer community radio station, 89.7 FM. Features old-time fiddle, old-time banjo, bluegrass fiddle, bluegrass banjo contests, old-time and non-traditional band contests. Clogging and square dancing. Performances held outdoors, with an indoor

---

MR = modern restrooms   RR = rustic restrooms   CO = camping on-site   CN = camping nearby   S = hot showers
RVO = RVs on-site   RVN = RVs nearby   HO = hookups on-site   HN = hookups nearby   M = motels nearby

venue available in case of rain. May 24: Square Dance, 8 pm.-midnight. May 25: Banjo and Fiddle Contest starts at noon, Band Contest starts at 7 p.m. Dance is $5 per person, children (under 13) free, 20% discount for advance sale to groups of 15 or more. Contests (both) are $8 per person, children (under 13) free. A, FF, RF, R, P (outdoors only), MR, RR, CO, CN, RVO, RVN, HO (limited), HN, M

Contact: Char Sweet, WVLS, P.O. Box 431, Monterey, VA 24465 • Phone: 540-468-2222 • Fax: 540-468-2223

MAURY RIVER FIDDLERS CONVENTION
June 20-22
Glen Maury Park, Buena Vista, VA

Since 1994. Annual attendance is 3,000. This festival showcases traditional bluegrass and old time music. Only string acoustic instruments are allowed on stage; no electrical instruments. Only songs and instruments from the public domain – no copyrighted music permitted. Features 14 music and dance competitions. Performances held both outdoors and indoors (large pavilion). Flatfoot dancing. Playground and swimming pool available for the children. Events are held all day and evening – hours vary. Tickets: $5 Thursday and Friday, $6 Saturday, $15 for contestants and season pass, children accompanied by adult admitted free. A, F, R, MR, RR, CO, CN, S, RVO, RVN, HO, HN, M

Contact: Joe Malloy, Maury River Fiddlers Convention, P.O. Box 702, Buena Vista, VA 24416 • Phone: 703-261-7321 or 800-555-8845

MOTHER'S DAY SHOWER OF STARS
May 9-11
American Legion Park, Culpeper, VA

Since 1993. This year's headliners include Boys From Indiana, Ralph Stanley, Country Gentlemen, Raymond Fairchild, Lost & Found, Larry Sparks. Past performers: Bill Monroe, Ralph Stanley, Larry Sparks, IIIrd Tyme Out, Lonesome River Band. All performances held outdoors. A covered area is available for the audience. Hours: Thursday 5:30 p.m.-11 p.m., Friday 1 p.m.-11 p.m., Saturday noon-11 p.m. Tickets: Thursday $12, Friday $20, Saturday $20. Advance ticket sales available. A, FF, RF, R, CC, RR, CO, RVN, HN, M

Contact: T.I. Gilbert, P.O. Box 227, Ruckersville, VA 22968 • Phone: 804-985-4727

OLD FIDDLERS CONVENTION
August 7-10
Felts Park, South Main Street, Galax, VA

Since 1934. Annual attendance is 30,000. The Old Fiddlers Convention features only traditional and bluegrass music of the old-time or public domain. No copyrighted music permitted. Musical competitions (all amateur), workshops, crafts

---

A = wheelchair accessible   I = interpreter for hearing impaired   F = food   FF = fast food   EF = ethnic food
VF = vegetarian food   RF = regional food   R = restaurants nearby   P = pets welcome   CC = credit cards

area, and competition clogging. All performances are held outdoors. A covered area is available for the audience. The festival starts at 6 p.m. each day. A four-day pass is $20. Wednesday and Thursday rates are $5 each day. Friday and Saturday rates are $7 each day. A, FF, R, MR, RR, CO, CN, S, RVN, HN, M

Contact: Tom Jones, Old Fiddlers Convention, P.O. Box 655, Galax, VA 24333-0655 • Phone: 540-236-8541 or 540-236-8681 • Fax: 540-236-8681 (call first)

SHENANDOAH APPLE BLOSSOM FESTIVAL
May 2-5
Winchester, VA

Since 1924. Annual attendance is 300,000. This festival offers a great time for the entire family with different activities for all happening throughout the event. From the pageantry of the Queen's coronation to the largest display of fire fighting equipment in the country to the much-celebrated Grand Feature Parade to the old-fashioned fun of "Weekend in the Park," this All-American community's celebration of a promising apple crops has something for everyone. Past performers include: Ralph Stanley, Navy Band's Country Current, Jim & Jesse, Mac Wiseman, Johnson Mountain Boys, Red and Murphy and Their Excellent Children, and Dalton Brill. Children's activities, crafts, and square dancing. Performances held both indoors and outdoors, with a tent available outdoors. Hours are 8 a.m.-midnight. Prices vary per day and event. Call to receive a brochure. A, FF, EF, RF, R, CC (no phone orders), RR, CN, M

Contact: Ben B. Dutton, Jr., Exec. Director, 135 North Cameron Street, Winchester, VA 22601 • Phone: 703-662-3863 • Fax: 703-622-7274

VIRGINIA FOLK MUSIC ASSOCIATION BLUEGRASS FESTIVAL
September 8
Mecklinburg Co-op Pavilion, Chase City, VA

Since 1957. Annual attendance is 4,000. Features bluegrass bands, fiddle, flat top, and mandolin music. Male & female vocalists, and junior entertainers. Musical competitions, workshops, children's activities. All performances held outdoors. A covered area is available for the audience. Hours: 11 am. until ??. Tickets: $6 adults, $1 children (under 12). A, FF, R, P, MR, CN, M

Contact: Joe Martin, President or Lois Clements, 1811 Wakefield Avenue, Colonial Heights, VA 23834 • Phone: 804-526-6092 (Joe) or 804-645-7419 (Lois)

MR = modern restrooms   RR = rustic restrooms   CO = camping on-site   CN = camping nearby   S = hot showers
RVO = RVs on-site   RVN = RVs nearby   HO = hookups on-site   HN = hookups nearby   M = motels nearby

Washington

DARRINGTON BLUEGRASS FESTIVAL
July 19-21
Darrington Music Park, Darrington, WA

Annual attendance is 4,000 to 6,000. Held in a beautiful 40 acre wooded park with a very large amphitheater. There is a breathtaking view of Whitehorse Mountain from the stage and arena. Whitehorse is a glacier peak with snow year round — truly phenomenal! Children's activities and crafts area. A dance area is available for anyone wishing to dance. All performances held outdoors. Past performers: Out of the Blue, Sawtooth Mountain Boys, City Limits, Side Saddle, Rural Delivery, Sam Hill. Hours: Friday 7 p.m.-11 p.m., Saturday 9 a.m.-11 p.m., Sunday 8 a.m.-9:30 p.m. Weekend pass is $25 with $10 camping fee for weekend. Friday $8, Saturday $10, Sunday $8. Advance ticket sales available. A, FF, R, RR, CO, RVO, M

Contact: Louie Ashe or Grover Jones or Birtha Nations, Annual Darrington Bluegrass Festival, P.O. Box 519, Darrington, WA 98241 • Phone: 360-436-0246 or 360-436-1006 or 360-436-1077

WINTERGRASS
February 22-25
Tacoma Sheraton Hotel, Tacoma, WA

Since 1994. Annual attendance is 3,500 per day. Wintergrass is an indoor winter bluegrass bash in elegant surroundings. With the run of at least 5 hotels, all night jamming, and over 50 bands and workshops, this event draws audiences and performers from all over the world. Fun and laughter are in plentiful supply. This year's headliners include Bill Monroe, Cox Family, Del McCoury, Chesapeake, Peter Rowan & The Rowan Brothers, Country Current (U.S. Navy Band), Laurie Lewis & Grant Street, Dry Branch Fire Squad, Ralph Stanley. Past performers: Bill Monroe, Nashville Bluegrass Band, J.D. Crowe, Tony Rice, Cox Family, Johnson Mountain Boys. Musical competitions, workshops, children's activities, crafts and dancing (Cajun and folk). All performances are held indoors. Hours are Thursday 6 p.m. through Sunday 4 p.m. Weekend passes: adults $75, seniors $65, kids $30. Thursday only $15, Friday only $35 (seniors $30), Saturday only $35 (seniors $30), Sunday only $25 (seniors $20). Discounted advance weekend passes available. A, I, FF, EF, VF, RF, R, MR, S, RVO, HO (limited), M

Contact: Rob Folsom or Earla Harding, Wintergrass, 3910 SE Salmonberry Road, Port Orchard, WA 98366 • Phone: 360-871-7354 • Fax: 360-871-4719

A = wheelchair accessible   I = interpreter for hearing impaired   F = food   FF = fast food   EF = ethnic food
VF = vegetarian food   RF = regional food   R = restaurants nearby   P = pets welcome   CC = credit cards

Wisconsin

CHIPPEWA VALLEY GOSPEL BLUEGRASS FESTIVAL
August 24-26
Living Waters Campground, Bruce, WI

Since 1990. Features gospel bluegrass and old-time gospel music. Past performers: Betty Jean Robinson, The Sullivan Family, The Village Singers, The Impacts. Open stage. Children's activities. All performances held outdoors. Hours: Friday 7 p.m.-11 pm., Saturday 10 a.m.-11 p.m., Sunday 9 a.m.-noon. Call for ticket prices. Advance ticket sales available. A, FF, RF, R, P, RR, CO, RVN, HN, M

Contact: Truman Stricklen, N7347 Highway 40, Bruce, WI 54819 • Phone: 715-868-2980 or 715-868-2987

SEVENTH ANNUAL MIDSUMMER IN THE NORTHWOODS BLUEGRASS FESTIVAL
July 24-28
Cozy Cove Restaurant & Tavern on Hwy. 51, Manitowish Waters, WI

Since 1990. Annual attendance is 350. Always held the last weekend in July, this festival in the Wisconsin Northwoods is a beautiful place to enjoy a bluegrass show. Emphasis is on traditional bluegrass music, but a portion of time is also allotted for Cajun, folk and old time music. Sit in the shade of the oaks and Norwegian pines, catch a little sun next to children making sand castles in the sand, or tap a few steps on the dance floor to the right of the stage. Meet the legends of bluegrass in the intimate confines of the Cozy Cove — you're among friends! This year's headliners: Jim and Jesse and The Virginia Boys, Dry Branch Fire Squad, Rarely Herd, Bill Jorgenson Bluegrass Ensemble, Bluegrass Survivors, and more. Past performers: Bill Monroe, Ralph Stanley, The Osborne Brothers, The Larkin Family, The Bob Lewis Family, Benny Martin, Alison Krauss, Claire Lynch, Laurie Lewis, and many more. Workshops, children's activities, crafts area, and dancing (folk and traditional). Performances held both indoors and outdoors. A covered area is available for the audience outdoors. Hours: 10 a.m.-midnight each day. Tickets: Thursday, Friday, Sunday $15; Saturday $20. Three-day pass $45. Four-day pass $48. Children $2. Seniors 10% discount. Advance ticket sales available. A, EF, VF, RF, R, MR, RR, CO, CN, S, RVO, RVN, HN, M

Contact: Jerry Florian, Northwoods Bluegrass Festival, Rt. 2, Box 23, Hwy. 51, Manitowish Waters, WI 54545 • Phone: 715-543-2166

MR = modern restrooms   RR = rustic restrooms   CO = camping on-site   CN = camping nearby   S = hot showers
RVO = RVs on-site   RVN = RVs nearby   HO = hookups on-site   HN = hookups nearby   M = motels nearby

Wyoming

High Plains Old-Time Country Music Show and Contest

April 27-28
Douglas High School Auditorium, Douglas, WY

Since 1985. Annual attendance is 300. The music at this event reflects country, folk and bluegrass roots using banjo, fiddle, guitar, vocals, piano, mandolin and a variety of other instruments. It offers the largest variety of categories for competition in the Rocky Mountain region including competitive categories for youth. Craft fair booths. Country-western dancing. All performances and events held indoors. Hours: 9 a.m. Saturday through 5 p.m. Sunday. Tickets: $5 general admission, $3 seniors and children (6-10 years old), children under 5 admitted free. Weekend pass: $12.50 general admission, $9 seniors and children. Craft fair is free. A, FF, R, MR, CN, RVO, RVN, HN, M

Contact: Vern & Barb Billingsley, Box 480, Douglas, WY 82633 • Phone: 307-358-9006 • Fax: 307-358-2950

Alberta

Blueberry Bluegrass & Country Music Festival

August 2-4
Spruce Grove, AB

Annual attendance is 2,800. This is the only bluegrass festival in the area and features excellent entertainment. Past performers: Bill Monroe. Workshops, children's activities, crafts area. All performances held outdoors. A covered area is available for the audience. Hours: Friday 8 p.m.-midnight, Saturday 1 p.m.-midnight, Sunday 11-11. Call for ticket information. Advance ticket sales available. A, F (breakfasts and dinners), FF, R, P (not in concert area), CC, MR, CO, RVN, HN, M

Contact: Shirley Skinner, P.O. Box 5151, Spruce Grove, AB T7X 3A3 • Phone: 403-963-5217

Shady Grove Bluegrass & Old Tyme Music Festival

August 17-19
Broadway Farm, 13 km east of Nanton, AB

Since 1990. Annual attendance is 2,500. This is a down-home family festival – small enough to treat everyone like family! Everyone is welcome to join in the jams. Features

---

| A = wheelchair accessible   I = interpreter for hearing impaired   F = food   FF = fast food   EF = ethnic food |
| VF = vegetarian food   RF = regional food   R = restaurants nearby   P = pets welcome   CC = credit cards |

bluegrass, old-time (traditional), country and strictly acoustic music. Past performers include: Special Consensus, Bluegrass, Etc., Jerusalem Ridge, Hot House Bluegrass Band, Katy Moffat. Workshops, children's activities, crafts area. Performances held both indoors and outdoors. Hours: Friday 7-11 p.m., Saturday 11:30 a.m.-11 p.m., Sunday 11:30 a.m.-5 p.m. Tickets: $35 for a weekend pass. Seniors and students $30. Advance ticket sales available. A, F (home cooking), FF, VF, R, P, MR, RR, S, RVO, RVN, M

Contact: Rosemary Wishart, P.O. Box 846, Nanton, AB T0L 1R0 • Phone: 403-646-2076 • Fax: 403-243-0472

British Columbia

BURNS LAKE BLUEGRASS & COUNTRY MUSIC FESTIVAL
June 29-July 1
Darter Ranch, 15 mi. S. on Hwy. 35, Burns Lake, BC

Since 1986. Annual attendance is 1,600. Features traditional bluegrass, contemporary bluegrass, and country music. 100% wholesome family entertainment. No alcohol permitted. 24-hour security and first aid. Held on a 420 acre ranch of rolling meadows, poplar groves, and duck ponds. This year's headliners: The Cox Family, Bill & Laurie Sky, Stew Clayton, and International Champion Yodeler Shirley Field. Past performers: Wild & Blue, The Gillis Brothers, Jerusalem Ridge, Stew Clayton, Queen's Bluegrass, Gospel Troubadours. All performances held outdoors. A covered area is available for the audience. Workshops, children's activities, crafts area, covered dance floor, barbecue dinner, pancake breakfast, homemade baking. Hours: Friday 5 p.m.-11 pm., Saturday noon-11 p.m., Sunday noon-9 p.m. Tickets: $42 weekend per person, $38 weekend senior, $34 weekend student, children under 12 admitted free. Advance ticket sales available. A, FF, RF, P, CC, RR, CO, RVO, RVN, HN, M

Contact: Richard Cannon, Burns Lake Festival, P.O. Box 113, Fraser Lake, BC V0J 1S0 • Phone: 604-699-8697 • Fax: 604-699-8535

GRANVILLE ISLAND BLUEGRASS FESTIVAL
May 4-5, May 11-12, May 18-20
Granville Island, Vancouver, BC

This festival is held in Vancouver at a unique heritage site that consists of a multicultural marketplace that sells arts and crafts, food and features theatre performances. Past performers: Kathy Kallick, Grier & Compton, Laurie Lewis, Blue Mule. Performances held both indoors and outdoors. A covered area is available for the audience outdoors. Crafts area and square dancing. Hours vary. A, FF, EF, VF, RF, R, MR, CO, M

Contact: Joanne Neighbour, Granville Island Bluegrass Festival, 1343 E. 14th Avenue, Vancouver, BC V5N 2C7 • Phone: 604-535-0351 • Fax: 604-535-0362

MR = modern restrooms   RR = rustic restrooms   CO = camping on-site   CN = camping nearby   S = hot showers
RVO = RVs on-site   RVN = RVs nearby   HO = hookups on-site   HN = hookups nearby   M = motels nearby

New Brunswick

MEMRAMCOOK VALLEY BLUEGRASS CAMPOUT
June 7-9
Rogersville, NB

Since 1990. This small but growing festival is operated by family and friends. It features bluegrass and old-time music performed by bands from the Maritime provinces. All performances held outdoors. A covered area is available for the audience. Traditional dancing. Hours: Friday 7 p.m.-11 p.m., Saturday noon-11 p.m., Sunday noon-4 p.m. Tickets: $23 (Canadian), $20 in advance. A, FF, R, P (on leash at all times), RR, CO, M (20 mi.)

Contact: Eddy Poirier, 76 Westbrook Circle, Moncton, NB E1E 2M1 • Phone: 506-384-8655

ROGERSVILLE HOMECOMING BLUEGRASS FESTIVAL
August 23-25
Rogersville, NB

Since 1993. This is a small but growing festival organized by a group of friends and family devoted to preserving bluegrass and old-time music. Features local bands from the New Brunswick area. All performances held outdoors. A covered area is available for the audience. Traditional dancing. Hours: Friday 7 p.m.-11 p.m., Saturday noon-11 p.m., Sunday noon-5 p.m. Tickets: $23 (Canadian), $20 in advance. A, FF, R, P (on leash at all times), RR, RVO, HO (electric only), M

Contact: Eddy Poirier, 76 Westbrook Circle, Moncton, NB E1E 2M1 • Phone: 506-384-8655

A = wheelchair accessible   I = interpreter for hearing impaired   F = food   FF = fast food   EF = ethnic food
VF = vegetarian food   RF = regional food   R = restaurants nearby   P = pets welcome   CC = credit cards

Nova Scotia

78TH CUMBERLAND CO. EXHIBITION & BLUEBERRY HARVEST FEST
August 27-31
Cumberland Co. Exhibition Fairgrounds, Oxford, NS

Since 1918. Annual attendance is 7,000. Features bluegrass (50%), country and western, rock, folk and maritime music. Past performers: Ellis Family Band, Atlantic String Show, Barry Hill Band, Ivan Hicks, Faye Strong. Home crafts, road rally, horse haul, talent search and livestock shows. Fine dining hall with excellent food and reasonable prices. Musical competitions, and children's activities. Performances held both indoors and outdoors. Hours: 10-10 each day. Tickets: $4.50 adults, children (12 and under) $2.50. F (full meals), FF, R, P, MR, M

Contact: Secretary/Manager, Harvest Fest, P.O. Box 516, Oxford, NS B0M 1P0 • Phone: 902-447-3285 or 902-447-3100

NOVA SCOTIA BLUEGRASS & OLD TIME MUSIC FESTIVAL
July 27-29
Beech Brook Campground, near Windsor, Ardoise, NS

Since 1971. Annual attendance is 2,000±. This is the oldest continuously operating festival of its kind in Canada, strictly adhering to acoustic music. Features acoustic bluegrass and old time music (no electric instruments or pick-ups allowed). Many intimate jam sessions. This year's headliner: The Del McCoury Band. Past performers: Bill Monroe, Bill Harrell, The Bluegrass Cardinals, Lost & Found, The Lynn Morris Band, and many more. Workshops and children's activities. All performances held outdoors. Hours: Friday evening, all day and evening Saturday, all day Sunday. Tentative ticket prices: $30 at the gate (includes field camping). Advance ticket sales available. A, FF, R, P (confined to campsite), RR, CO, S, RVN, HN, M

Contact: Wilson Moore, 119 Victoria St. W., Amherst, NS B4H 1C7 • Phone: 902-667-9629

MR = modern restrooms   RR = rustic restrooms   CO = camping on-site   CN = camping nearby   S = hot showers
RVO = RVs on-site   RVN = RVs nearby   HO = hookups on-site   HN = hookups nearby   M = motels nearby

January

January 12-13
  • Dixieland Bluegrass Monthly "Pickin & Grinin," Waldo, FL

January 12-14
  • Circle Of Friends Bluegrass Festival, Butler, PA

January 13-15
  • The Hawkeye Special Bluegrass Festival, Bettendorf, IA

January 18-21
  Yee Haw Junction Bluegrass Festival, Yee Haw Junction, FL

January 19-20
  • Winter Festival Bluegrass in Super Class, Perrysburg, OH

January 19-21
  • "Colorado River Country" Music Festival, Blythe, CA

January 20
  • Southeast Texas Bluegrass Music Association Jam & Show, Sour Lake, TX

January 26-28
  • Winter Indoor Bluegrass Festival, Qunicy, IL

February

February 8-11
  • The Winter Bluegrass Festival & Conference on Western Bluegrass, San Jose, CA

February 9-10
  • Dixieland Bluegrass Monthly "Pickin & Grinin," Waldo, FL

February 9-11
  • Everglades Bluegrass Convention, North Miami Beach, FL

February 11
  • 4th Ocean County Bluegrass Festival, Waretown, NJ (snow date February 18)

February 16-17
  • Bluegrass Get-A-Way, Fremont, OH

February 16-18
  • 18th Annual TSBA Winter Bluegrass Music Festival, Hannibal, MO
  • Colorado Mid-Winter Bluegrass Festival, Fort Collins, CO
  • Dixieland Bluegrass Family Reunion, Waldo, FL
  • Tater Hill Reunion, Arcadia, FL

February 17
• Southeast Texas Bluegrass Music Association Jam & Show, Sour Lake, TX

February 22-25
• Wintergrass, Tacoma, WA

February 23-25
• The Gateway City Bluegrass Festival, St. Louis, MO

February 24
• Star Fiddler's Convention, Biscoe, NC

March

March 1-2
• Asheville Bluegrass Under The Stars, Asheville, NC

March 2
• Acoustic Extraordinaire, Hattiesburg, MS

March 7-10
• 1996 Kissimmee Kiwanis Bluegrass Festival, Kissimmee, FL

March 8-9
• Cousin Jake Memorial Bluegrass Festival, Etowah, TN
• Dixieland Bluegrass Monthly "Pickin & Grinin," Waldo FL

March 8-10
• Northern Illinois in Naperville Bluegrass Festival, Naperville, IL
• The Indy Classic Bluegrass Festival, Indianapolis, IN

March 14-17
• Annual Sunshine State Bluegrass Festival, Punta Gorda, FL
• Pines Bluegrass Festival, South Fallsburg, NY

March 15-17
• Rib Rustlers Bluegrass Campout, Ft. Davis, TX

March 16
• Southeast Texas Bluegrass Music Association Jam & Show, Sour Lake, TX

March 22
• South Mississippi Bluegrass Jamboree, Runnelstown, MS

March 26-30
• Picking Around The Campfire, Texarkana, TX

March 29-30
• 2nd Annual Bluegrass in Luxury / Ralph Stanley's Birthday Celebration, Hudson, OH

March 29-31
- 10th Annual Bluegrass Music Weekend, Burlington, IA
- Florida's Withlacoochee River Bluegrass Jamboree, Dunnellon, FL

April

April 5-6
- 29th Semi-Annual Bluegrass Superjam, Cullman, AL

April 11-14
- Bluegrass Music Festival, Live Oak, FL

April 12-13
- Dixieland Bluegrass Monthly "Pickin & Grinin," Waldo, FL

April 13
- Mississippi Regional Pizza Hut International Bluegrass Showdown, Hattiesburg, MS

April 18-20
- Plum Creek Park Bluegrass Festival, Dew, TX

April 20
- Jacksonian Days, Scottsville, KY
- Southeast Texas Bluegrass Music Association Jam & Show, Sour Lake, TX

April 23-27
- Picking Around The Campfire, Texarkana, TX

April 25-28
- Merle Fest '96, Wilkesboro, NC
- Tres Rios 12th Annual Spring Bluegrass Festival, Glen Rose, TX

April 26-27
- Old York USA Annual Bluegrass Festival, Oakman, AL

April 27
- Swayed Pines Folk Festival, Collegeville, MN (call to verify)

April 27-28
- High Plains Old-Time Country Music Show & Contest, Douglas, WY

May

May 2-4
- 9th Annual Lewis Family Homecoming & Bluegrass Festival, Lincolnton, GA

May 2-5
- Gettysburg Bluegrass Festival, Gettysburg, PA
- Shenandoah Apple Blossom Festival, Winchester, VA

May 3-4
- 3rd Annual Park City Bluegrass Festival, Park City, KS
- Twin Oaks Park Bluegrass Convention, Hoboken, GA

May 4-5
- Granville Island Bluegrass Festival, Vancouver, BC

May 5
- Pine Barren's Festival, Waretown, NJ

May 9-11
- Mother's Day Shower of Stars, Culpeper, VA

May 10-11
- Dixieland Bluegrass Monthly "Pickin & Grinin," Waldo, FL
- Nine Mile Volunteer Fire Co. Bluegrass Festival, Pikeville, TN

May 11-12
- Granville Island Bluegrass Festival, Vancouver, BC

May 12
- Central Texas Bluegrass Association's Spring Music Festival, Austin, TX

May 16-18
- Central Virginia Family Bluegrass Music Festival, Amelia, VA

May 17-18
- Country Stage Bluegrass Festival, Nova, OH
- Sparks Family's 5th Annual Bluegrass Festival, Belmont, MS

May 17-19
- 9th Annual Spring Gulch Folk Festival, New Holland, PA
- Dixieland Bluegrass Family Reunion, Waldo, FL

May 18
- Southeast Texas Bluegrass Music Association Jam & Show, Sour Lake, TX

May 18-20
- Granville Island Bluegrass Festival, Vancouver, BC

May 19
- 36th Topanga Banjo & Fiddle Contest Dance & Folk Arts Festival, Agoura, CA

May 23-26
- Bass Mountain Music Park's Annual Memorial Day Festival, Burlington, NC
- Bluegrass Jamboree, Glen Rose, TX
- Dixon Bluegrass Pickin' Time, Dixon, MO
- Hebron Pines Bluegrass Festival, Hebron, ME
- Strange Family Spring Bluegrass Festival, Texarkana, TX

May 24-25
- Highland Bluegrass Festival, Monterey, VA
- The Vic Rhodes Traditional Music Festival, Williston, TN

May 24-26
- 2nd Annual Lone Wolf Bluegrass Festival, Colorado City, TX
- 2nd Annual Memorial Day Bluegrass Festival, Burlington, IA
- Kern County Bluegrass Festival and Craft Fair, Bakersfield, CA
- Ole Time Fiddler's & Bluegrass Festival, Union Grove, NC

May 24-27
- Memorial Day Weekend, Live Oak, FL

May 25
- Riverwalk Bluegrass Festival, Augusta, GA

May 25-26
- 4th Annual Northern Neck Bluegrass Festival, Warsaw, VA

May 30-June 1
- Graves Mountain Festival of Music, Syria, VA
- Hamby Mountain 16th Annual Spring Bluegrass Festival, Baldwin, GA

May 31-June 1
- Bluff Creek Bluegrass Festival, Phil Campbell, AL
- Coke Ovens Bluegrass Festival, Dunlap, TN

May 31-June 2
- 1996 Seventh Annual Bluegrass on the River, Pueblo, CO
- Hunter Creek Kickoff, Palmer, AK
- Mountain Top Spring Bluegrass Festival, Tarentum, PA

June

June 5-8
- Sanders Family Bluegrass Festival, McAlester, OK

June 7-8
- Dixieland Bluegrass Monthly "Pickin & Grinin," Waldo, FL
- Foggy Hollow Bluegrass Gatherin', Webster's Chapel, AL
- Official Indiana Pickin' & Fiddlin' Contest, Petersburg, IN

June 7-9
- 1000 Islands Bluegrass Festival, Clayton, NY
- Memramcook Valley Bluegrass Campout, Rogersville, NB
- Sugar Creek Bluegrass Festival, Blue Ridge, GA

June 8
- Fiddle Fest '96, Wooster, OH

June 9
- Annual Willow Metro Park Bluegrass Festival, Flat Rock, MI

June 13-15
- Christopher Run Bluegrass Festival, Mineral, VA

June 13-16
- 21st Annual CBA Father's Day Bluegrass Festival, Grass Valley, CA
- Blistered Fingers 6th Annual Family Bluegrass Music Festival, Sidney, ME
- HOBA Bluegrass Festival, West Plains, MO

June 14-16
- Eastern Shore Bluegrass Association 16th Annual Festival, Harrington, DE

June 15
- Southeast Texas Bluegrass Music Association Jam & Show, Sour Lake, TX

June 19-24
- National Oldtime Fiddlers' Contest, Weiser, ID

June 20-22
- 22nd Annual Dahlonega Bluegrass Festival, Dahlonega, GA
- Maury River Fiddlers Convention, Buena Vista, VA

June 20-23
- Bean Blossom Bluegrass Festival, Bean Blossom, IN

June 21-22
- Airport Gospel Bluegrass '96, Dayton, OH
- Maple City Bluegrass Festival, Norwalk, OH
- Nine Mile-Edmons Family Bluegrass Festival, Pikeville, TN

June 28-29
- Grayson County Old-Time and Bluegrass Fiddlers Convention, Elk Creek, VA
- Rosine 23rd Annual Bluegrass Homecoming, Hartford, KY

June 28-30
- 19th Annual Grantsville Days, Grantsville, MD
- Black Hills Bluegrass Festival, Rapid City, SD

June 29-July 1
- Burns Lake Bluegrass & Country Music Festival, Burns Lake, BC

June (call for exact dates)
- 20th Annual Pickin' In The Pines Bluegrass Day, Northampton, MA
- Telluride Bluegrass Festival, Telluride, CO

July

July 3-7
- Sally Mountain 10th Annual Bluegrass Festival, Queen City, MO

July 4-7
- Comer Brothers Bluegrass Festival, Darlington, MD
- Hunter Creek Bluegrass Classic, Palmer, AK
- Jersey Town Bluegrass Festival, Jerseytown, PA
- Lively Liberty Festivities, Live Oak, FL

July 5-6
- Smithville Fiddlers Jamboree & Crafts Festival, Smithville, TN

July 5-7
- Musicians Rendezvous, Columbus, MT
- Old Joe Clark Bluegrass Festival, Renfro Valley, KY

July 10-13
- Elks Dixie Bluegrass Festival, Hattiesburg, MS

July 11-14
- Doyle Lawson and Quicksilver's Bluegrass Festival, Denton, NC

July 12-13
- Dixieland Bluegrass Monthly "Pickin & Grinin,"Waldo, FL

July 12-14
- 7th Annual Canyon Country Bluegrass Festival, Wellsboro, PA
- Basin Bluegrass Festival, Brandon, VT
- Summer Bluegrass Festival 1996, Irvine, CA

July 13
- Boulder Folk and Bluegrass Festival, Boulder, CO

July 13-14
- Bitterroot Valley Bluegrass Festival, Hamilton, MT

July 17-21
- McCullough Park Family Bluegrass Festival, Chillicothe, MO

July 18-20
- 13th Annual Mineral Bluegrass Festival, Mineral, VA
- Northeastern Ohio Bluegrass Festival, Bristolville, OH

July 18-21
- Peaceful Valley Bluegrass Festival, Shinhopple, NY
- Winterhawk Bluegrass Festival, Ancramdale, NY

July 19-20
- Official Kentucky State Championship Old-Time Fiddlers Contest Inc., Leitchfield, KY

July 19-21
- Darrington Bluegrass Festival, Darrington, WA

July 20
- Friendsville Fiddler's & Banjo Contest, Friendsville, MD
- South Alabama Bluegrass Convention & Fiddler's Championship, Atmore, AL
- Southeast Texas Bluegrass Music Association Jam & Show, Sour Lake, TX

July 20-21
- Hayseed "Mostly" Bluegrass Festival, Franconia, NH
- Old Bedford Village Bluegrass Festival, Bedford, PA

July 24-28
- Seventh Annual Midsummer In The Northwoods Bluegrass Festival, Manitowish Waters, WI

July 25-27
- Bluegrass Classic at Frontier Ranch, Columbus, OH

July 25-28
- 18th Annual Salt River Bluegrass Festival, Oil City, MI

July 26-27
- Rick & Carol's Country Music & Bluegrass Festival, Fort Ann, NY
- Snyder Bluegrass Festival, Lawrenceburg, MO

July 26-28
- Backbone Bluegrass Festival, Strawberry Point, IA
- Sugar Creek Bluegrass Festival, Blue Ridge, GA

July 27-28
- Connecticut Family Folk Festival, Hartford, CT

July 27-29
- Nova Scotia Bluegrass & Old Time Music Festival, Ardoise, NS

July 29
- 24th Annual East Benton Fiddlers Convention, East Benton, ME

July (call for exact dates)
- St. Mary Park Bluegrass Festival, Monroe, MI
- Summer Swamp Stomp, Tallahassee, FL

August

August 1-3
- 69th Annual Mountain Dance & Folk Festival, Asheville NC
- Bluegrass in the Park, Henderson, KY

August 2-3
- Carter Family Memorial Music Festival, Hiltons, VA
- Nine Mile-Edmons Family Bluegrass Festival, Pikeville, TN

August 2-4
- 4th Annual Pemi Valley Bluegrass Festival, Campton NH
- Blueberry Bluegrass & Country Music Festival, Spruce Grove, AB
- Minnesota Bluegrass & Old-Time Music Festival, Zimmerman, MN
- Rocky Grass – The Rocky Mountain Bluegrass Festival, Lyons, CO

August 3
- 16th Annual Old Fiddlers Picnic, Lancaster, PA

August 3-4
- Frog Bottom Bluegrass Festival, Cornersville, TN
- Stoney Run Bluegrass Festival, Leroy, IN
- The Sparks Family's 13th Annual Bluegrass Festival, Belmont, MS

August 3-5
- Bill Knowlton's Bluegrass Ramble Picnic, Sandy Creek, NY

August 7-10
- Kahoka Festival of Bluegrass Music, Kahoka, MO
- Old Fiddlers Convention, Galax, VA

August 7-18
- Georgia Mountain Fair, Hiawassee, GA

August 8-11
- HOBA Bluegrass Festival – Heart of the Ozarks, West Plains, MO
- Little Margaret's Bluegrass & Old-Time Country Music Festival, Leonardtown, MD
- Wise Owl Mountain Jam '96, Ulysses, PA

August 9-10
- 4th Annual Lawrenceburg Bluegrass Festival, Lawrenceburg, IN
- Banner Bluegrass Festival, Banner, MS
- Bell Witch Bluegrass Competition, Adams, TN
- Dixieland Bluegrass Monthly "Pickin & Grinin," Waldo, FL

August 9-11
- Spring Holler Bluegrass Festival, Dunnville, KY

August 11
- Founders Title Company Folk & Bluegrass Festival, Park City, UT

August 15-17
- Central Virginia Family Bluegrass Music Festival, Amelia, VA

August 15-18
- Money Creek Haven Country-Bluegrass Festival, Houston, MN
- Southern Michigan No. 1 Annual Bluegrass Festival, Leslie, MI

August 16-17
- Country Stage Bluegrass Festival, Nova, OH

August 16-18
- Oxford County Bluegrass Festival, S. Paris, ME
- Pickin' By The River, Grassy, MO
- St. Lawrence Valley Bluegrass Festival, Gouverneur, NY

August 17
- Southeast Texas Bluegrass Music Association Jam & Show, Sour Lake, TX

August 17-18
- Rockome Gardens Bluegrass Festival, Arcola, IL
- Sawlog 'N' Strings Bluegrass & Folk Festival, Dodge City, KS

August 17-19
- Shady Grove Bluegrass & Old Tyme Music Festival, Nanton, AB

August 18
- Western New England Old-Time & Bluegrass Music Championships, Sheffield, MA

August 22-24
- 14th Annual Cherokee Bluegrass Festival, Cherokee, NC

August 22-25
- Gettysburg Bluegrass Festival, Gettysburg, PA

August 23-24
- Smoky Mountain Fiddlers Convention, Loudon, TN

August 23-25
- 20th Annual Bluegrass Festival, Pioneer, OH
- Rogersville Homecoming Bluegrass Festival, Rogersville, NB

August 24
- 18th Annual Humboldt Folklife Festival, Eureka, CA
- Union Grove Music Festival, Union Grove, NC

August 24-26
- Chippewa Valley Gospel Bluegrass Festival, Bruce, WI

August 24-September 1
- Blue Mountain Gospel Music Festival, Kempton, PA

August 27-31
- 78th Cumberland Co. Exhibition & Blueberry Harvest Fest, Oxford, NS

August 29-September 1
- Dixon Bluegrass Pickin' Time, Dixon, MO
- Strange Family Fall Bluegrass Festival, Texarkana, TX

August 30-September 1
- 17th Annual Cajun & Bluegrass Music Festival, Escoheag, RI
- 19th Annual Thomas Point Beach Bluegrass Festival, Brunswick, ME
- 20th Annual Salmon Lake Park Bluegrass Festival, Grapeland, TX
- 25th Annual Delaware Valley Bluegrass Festival, Woodstown, NJ
- Bass Mountain Music Park's Annual Labor Day Festival, Burlington, NC
- New Coon Creek Girls Bluegrass Festival, Renfro Valley, KY
- Wrench Wranch Bluegrass Roundup, Coventryville, NY

August 30-September 2
- Labor Day Weekend, Live Oak, FL

August 31-September 1
- Annual Missouri River Bluegrass & Old Time Music Festival, near Washburn, ND

August 31-September 2
- Mountain Top Fall Bluegrass Festival, Tarentum, PA

September

September 1-2
- Berlin Community Grove Bluegrass Festival, Berlin, PA

September 4-7
- McCullough Park Family Bluegrass Festival, Chillicothe, MO

September 6-7
- Grand Caverns 11th Annual Bluegrass Festival, Grottoes, VA
- Twin Oaks·Park Bluegrass Convention, Hoboken, GA

September 7-8
- Fall Jamboree, Millbridge, NC

September 8
- 5th Ocean County Bluegrass Festival, Waretown, NJ
- Virginia Folk Music Association Bluegrass Festival, Chase City, VA

September 12-15
- Tres Rios 12th Annual Fall Bluegrass Festival, Glen Rose, TX

September 13-14
- Dixieland Bluegrass Monthly "Pickin & Grinin," Waldo, FL

September 13-15
- Bean Blossom Bluegrass Festival, Bean Blossom, IN
- Mohican Bluegrass Festival, near Loudonville, OH

September 15
- 7th Annual Andalusia Bluegrass Day, Andalusia, PA

September 17-21
- Poppy Mountain Bluegrass Fest, Morehead, KY

September 19-22
- 25th Annual Walnut Valley Festival & International Flatpicking Championships, Winfield, KS

September 20-21
- Country Stage Bluegrass Festival, Nova, OH
- Nine Mile Volunteer Fire Co. Bluegrass Festival, Pikeville, TN

September 20-22
- IBMA Bluegrass Fan Fest '96, Owensboro, KY
- Lazy River Bluegrass Festival, Gardiner, NY
- Smoky Mountain Gospel Singing, Sevierville, TN

September 21
- Southeast Texas Bluegrass Music Association Jam & Show, Sour Lake, TX

September 21-23
- Hillside Bluegrass Festival, Cochran, GA

September 24-28
- Picking Around The Campfire, Texarkana, TX

September 26-28
- Hamby Mountain 16th Annual Fall Bluegrass Festival, Baldwin, GA
- Lakeview Bluegrass Music Festival, Waldron, AR
- Plum Creek Park Bluegrass Festival, Dew, TX

September 26-29
- 13th Annual Arcadia Bluegrass Festival, Upperco, MD
- Original Ozark Folk Festival, Eureka Springs, AR

September 27-28
- Bluff Creek Bluegrass Festival, Phil Campbell, AL
- Foggy Hollow Bluegrass Gatherin', Webster's Chapel, AL

September 27-29
- Eagle Mountain Bluegrass & Old Tyme Country Music Festival, Van Horn, TX

September 28
- 4th Annual Berlin Fiddler's Convention, Berlin, MD

September 28-29
- Myrtle Creek Bluegrass Festival, Myrtle Creek, OR

September (call for exact date)
- Annual Appalachian Dumplin' Festival, Winfield, TN

October

October 4-5
- Tennessee Valley Old Time Fiddlers Convention, Athens, AL

October 4-6
- Bluegrass Jamboree, Glen Rose, TX
- Butterwood Bluegrass Festival, Littleton, NC

October 5
- Bluegrass Festival & Children's Fall Festival, Archbold, OH

October 6
- 3rd Annual Sunday Afternoon Bluegrass Festival, Cary, NC

October 10-13
- 29th Annual Autumn Glory Festival, Oakland, MD
- Museum of Appalachia's Tennessee Fall Homecoming, Norris, TN

October 11-12
- Dixieland Bluegrass Monthly "Pickin & Grinin," Waldo, FL

October 11-13
- Cumberland Mountain Fall Festival, Middlesboro, KY
- Sugar Creek Bluegrass Festival, Blue Ridge, GA

October 12-13
- It's Not Almost It Is! Paradise! Bluegrass Festival, Mackinac Island, MI

October 18-20
- Dixieland Bluegrass Family Reunion, Waldo, FL

October 19
- King Oyster's Bluegrass Revue, Leonardtown, MD
- Southeast Texas Bluegrass Music Association Jam & Show, Sour Lake, TX

October 22-26
- Boo Grass Picking Around the Campfire, Texarkana, TX

October 24-26
• Bluegrass Music in the Fall, Live Oak, FL

October 25-27
• Spring Creek Bluegrass Club Festival, Bellville, TX

October 31-November 2
• Florida's Withlacoochee River Bluegrass Jamboree, Dunnellon, FL

November

November 1-2
• 30th Semi-Annual Bluegrass Superjam, Cullman, AL

November 1-3
• 10th Annual Fall Bluegrass Festival, Ft. Madison, IA
• Fiddlers' Festival, Renfro Valley, KY

November 8-9
• Dixieland Bluegrass Monthly "Pickin & Grinin," Waldo, FL

November 8-10
• 4 Corner States Bluegrass Festival, Wickenburg, AZ
• Greater Downstate Indoor Bluegrass Festival & Guitar Show, Decatur, IL

November 10
• Homeplace Festival, Waretown, NJ

November 15-17
• 15th Land of Mark Twain Music Festival, Hannibal, MO

November 16
• Southeast Texas Bluegrass Music Association Jam & Show, Sour Lake, TX

November 16-17
• Bluegrass Primetime Pre-Holiday Festival, Sandusky, OH

November 21-24
• New Star Rising, Live Oak, FL

November 28-30
• 27th Annual South Carolina State Bluegrass Festival, Myrtle Beach, SC

November 28-December 1
• Thanksgiving Harvest Weekend, Live Oak, FL

December

December 13-14
  • Dixieland Bluegrass Monthly "Pickin & Grinin," Waldo, FL

December 21
  • Southeast Texas Bluegrass Music Association Jam & Show, Sour Lake, TX

December 31
  • First Night Out, Toledo, OH

Late Arrivals

HUNTER CREEK KICKOFF
May 31-June 2
Mile 8.2 Knik River Road, Palmer, AK

Since 1992. Annual attendance is 800 to 1,000. Features bluegrass, gospel, Irish and folk music in a picture postcard setting in Alaska. Festival site is at the foot of the Knik Glacier. Parking lot picking and jams around the clock. This year's headliners: Ginger Boatwright, Sam Hill Band, Northern River, Spur Hiway Spankers, and 30+ bands. All performances held outdoors. A covered area is available for the audience. Workshops, children's activities, crafts area, and dancing (clogging). Hours are 12-12 daily. Tickets: $20 weekend pass, $10 day rate, children under 12 and seniors free. Advance ticket sales available. A, FF, EF, RF, P, CC, MR, RR, CO, CN, S, RVO

Contact: Steve McDermott, Hunter Creek Kickoff, 3600 Doroshin, Anchorage, AK 99516 • Phone: 907-345-2247 • Fax: 907-659-6787

HUNTER CREEK BLUEGRASS CLASSIC
July 4-7
Mile 8.2 Knik River Road, Palmer, AK

Since 1991. Annual attendance is 1,000 to 1,200. Held in a beautiful setting in Alaska's wilderness, the festival site is between two mountain ranges at the foot of Knik Glacier. Features great bluegrass, gospel, Irish and folk music. This year's headliners: Bluegrass Patriots, Doug Dillard Band, Bluegrass Etc., Gale Force, Talkeetna Travelers, Frontier Spirit, Ginger Boatwright, with 30+ bands. Past performers: John McEuen, Steve Kaufman. All performances held outdoors. A covered area is available for the audience. Workshops, children's activities, and crafts area. Dancing includes clogging and square dancing. Hours are 12-12 daily. Tickets: $25 weekend pass, $10 day rate, children under 12 and seniors free. Advance ticket sales available. A, FF, EF, RF, P, CC, MR, RR, CO, CN, S, RVO

Contact: Steve McDermott, Hunter Creek Bluegrass Classic, 3600 Doroshin, Anchorage, AK 99516 • Phone: 907-345-2247 • Fax: 907-659-6787

ORDER NOW!

Bluegrass Music Festivals
1997 Guide for U.S. & Canada

Available mid-November 1996

Each entry includes:
• Date   • Location   • Contact Person
• Phone Number   • Valuable Information

Also Available:

Folk & Traditional Music Festivals
1997 Guide for U.S. & Canada

The Book Publishing Company
PO Box 99
Summertown, TN 38483

for MasterCard and VISA orders call

1-800-695-2241

Please send me ____ copy(s) of the **Bluegrass Music Festivals 1997 Guide for U.S. & Canada at $12.45 *per book* ($9.95 + $2.50 shipping).**

Please send me ____ copy(s) of the **Folk & Traditional Music Festivals 1997 Guide for U.S. & Canada at $13.45 *per book* ($10.95 + $2.50 shipping).**

Canadian orders: Enclose a Canadian postal union money order in U.S. funds. Shipping for Canadian orders is $3.00 *per book.*

Name _____

Address _____

City, ST, Zip _____

Checks payable to: Book Publishing Co., PO Box 99, Summertown, TN 38483